James Hadley Chase and The Murder Room

>>> This title is part of The Murder Room, our series dedicated to making available out-of-print or hard-to-find titles by classic crime writers.

Crime fiction has always held up a mirror to society. The Victorians were fascinated by sensational murder and the emerging science of detection; now we are obsessed with the forensic detail of violent death. And no other genre has so captivated and enthralled readers.

Vast troves of classic crime writing have for a long time been unavailable to all but the most dedicated frequenters of second-hand bookshops. The advent of digital publishing means that we are now able to bring you the backlists of a huge range of titles by classic and contemporary crime writers, some of which have been out of print for decades.

From the genteel amateur private eyes of the Golden Age and the femmes fatales of pulp fiction, to the morally ambiguous hard-boiled detectives of mid twentieth-century America and their descendants who walk our twenty-first century streets, The Murder Room has it all. >>>

The Murder Room
Where Criminal Minds Meet

themurderroom.com

T0352486

James Hadley Chase (1906–1985)

Born René Brabazon Raymond in London, the son of a British colonel in the Indian Army, James Hadley Chase was educated at King's School in Rochester, Kent, and left home at the age of 18. He initially worked in book sales until, inspired by the rise of gangster culture during the Depression and by reading James M. Cain's *The Postman Always Rings Twice*, he wrote his first novel, *No Orchids for Miss Blandish*. Despite the American setting of many of his novels, Chase (like Peter Cheyney, another hugely successful British noir writer) never lived there, writing with the aid of maps and a slang dictionary. He had phenomenal success with the novel, which continued unabated throughout his entire career, spanning 45 years and nearly 90 novels. His work was published in dozens of languages and over thirty titles were adapted for film. He served in the RAF during World War II, where he also edited the RAF Journal. In 1956 he moved to France with his wife and son; they later moved to Switzerland, where Chase lived until his death in 1985.

By James Hadley Chase
(published in the Murder Room)

No Orchids for Miss Blandish (1939)
Eve (1945)
More Deadly Than the Male (1946)
Mission to Venice (1954)
Mission to Siena (1955)
Not Safe to Be Free (1958)
Shock Treatment (1959)
Come Easy – Go Easy (1960)
What's Better Than Money? (1960)
Just Another Sucker (1961)
I Would Rather Stay Poor (1962)
A Coffin from Hong Kong (1962)
Tell it to the Birds (1963)
One Bright Summer Morning (1963)
The Soft Centre (1964)
You Have Yourself a Deal (1966)
Have This One on Me (1967)
Well Now, My Pretty (1967)
Believed Violent (1968)
An Ear to the Ground (1968)
The Whiff of Money (1969)
The Vulture Is a Patient Bird (1969)
Like a Hole in the Head (1970)

An Ace Up My Sleeve (1971)
Want to Stay Alive? (1971)
Just a Matter of Time (1972)
You're Dead Without Money (1972)
Have a Change of Scene (1973)
Knock, Knock! Who's There? (1973)
Goldfish Have No Hiding Place (1974)
So What Happens to Me? (1974)
The Joker in the Pack (1975)
Believe This, You'll Believe Anything (1975)
Do Me a Favour – Drop Dead (1976)
I Hold the Four Aces (1977)
My Laugh Comes Last (1977)
Consider Yourself Dead (1978)
You Must Be Kidding (1979)
A Can of Worms (1979)
Try This One for Size (1980)
You Can Say That Again (1980)
Hand Me a Fig-Leaf (1981)
Have a Nice Night (1982)
We'll Share a Double Funeral (1982)
Not My Thing (1983)
Hit Them Where It Hurts (1984)

An Ear to the Ground

James Hadley Chase

An Orion book

Copyright © Hervey Raymond 1968

The right of James Hadley Chase to be identified as the author of this work has been asserted in accordance with the Copyright, Designs and Patents Act 1988.

This edition published by
The Orion Publishing Group Ltd
Orion House
5 Upper St Martin's Lane
London WC2H 9EA

An Hachette UK company
A CIP catalogue record for this book is available from the British Library

ISBN 978 1 4719 0364 9

www.orionbooks.co.uk

CHAPTER ONE

I had this story from Al Barney, a beer-sodden beach-comber who haunts the waterfront of Paradise City, always on the look out for a sucker to buy him a beer.

At one time, so I was told, Al Barney was the best skin diver on the coast. He had picked up a lot of money teaching diving, spearing sharks and laying the wives of the rich tourists who infest this coast in the season. But the beer ruined him.

Al was an enormous man, weighing around three hundred and fifty pounds with a beer belly on him that rested like a balloon on his knees when he sat down. He was around sixty-three years of age, burned mahogany brown by years in the sun, balding, with an egg-shaped head, steely, small green eyes, a mouth that reminded me of a Red Snapper and a flat nose that spread half over his face from a punch he had had – so he told me – from an unreasonable husband who had caught him in the hay with his wife.

I had written a novel that had clicked lucky, and I had now enough spending money to escape the cold in New York, so I had come down to Paradise City which is on the Florida coast, knowing I could well afford to spend a month there before I got back to more work. I checked in at the Spanish Bay Hotel: probably the best and most de luxe of all the hotels in Florida. It only catered for fifty guests and offered a service that fully justified the cost of the final tab.

Jean Dulac, the manager of the hotel, a tall handsome man with impeccable manners and the polished charm that is unique to the French, had read my book. It had made a hit with him, and one evening as I was sitting on the floodlit terrace after one of those magnificent meals the Spanish Bay Hotel always provided, Dulac joined me.

He told me about Al Barney.

Smiling, he said, "He's our very special local character. He knows everyone, knows everything about this City. It might amuse you to talk to him. If you are looking for material, you'll certainly get something from him."

After a week of swimming, eating too much, lazing in the sun and fooling around with a number of girls with beautiful bodies but no minds, I remembered what Dulac had told me about Al Barney. Sooner or later, I would have to get down to another book. I had no ideas, so I drove over to the Neptune Tavern on the oily waterfront where the sponge fishing boats docked and found Barney.

He was sitting outside the Neptune Tavern on a bollard, a can of beer in his hand, staring moodily at the boats as they came and went.

I introduced myself, telling him that Dulac had mentioned his name.

"Mr Dulac? Yeah ... a gentleman. Glad to meet you." He extended a big grimy paw that was as soft and as yielding as a steel hawser. "So you're a writer?"

I said I was.

He finished the can of beer, then tossed it into the harbour.

"Let's go get us a drink," he said and heaved his enormous bulk off the bollard. He led me across the quay and into the gloomy, dirty Neptune Tavern. A coloured barman grinned at him as we came in, his eyes sparkling. I could see from his expression that he knew Al had landed yet another sucker.

We drank and talked of this and that, then after his third beer, Al said, "Would you be looking for a story, mister?"

"I'm always looking for a story."

2

"Do you want to hear about the Esmaldi diamonds?" Al peered hopefully at me.

"I'll listen," I said. "What have I to lose?"

Al smiled. He had an odd smile. The small Red Snapper mouth curved up. He looked as if he were smiling, but when I looked into the small green eyes, there was no smile there.

"I'm like a beat up old Ford," he said. "I go five miles to the gallon." He looked at his empty glass. "Keep me filled up, and I go like a bird."

I went over to the grinning barman and got that problem straightened out. Al talked for four solid hours. Every time his glass was empty, the barman came over with a refill. I've seen drinking in my time, but nothing to match this.

"I've been around this little City now for fifty years," Al said, staring at the beer in his glass with its white frothy head. "I'm a guy with his ear to the ground. I listen. I get told. I put two and two together. I've got contacts with the cops, the newspapers, the guys who know all the dirt . . . they talk to me." He took a long drink of beer and belched gently. "You understand? I know the stoolies, the jail birds, the whores, the black boys who are always invisible, but who have ears. I listen. You get the photo, mister? A guy with his ear to the ground."

I said I got it and what was all this about the Esmaldi diamonds?

Al put his hand under his dirty sweat shirt and scratched his enormous paunch. He finished his beer, then looked at the barman who grinned happily and came over to supply the refill. These two worked together like a piston and rod.

"The Esmaldi diamonds? You want to hear about them?"

"Why not?"

He regarded me, his little green eyes flinty.

"You could turn it into a story?"

"I don't know ... I could ... how can I say without hearing about it?"

He nodded his bald, egg-shaped head.

"Yeah. Well, if you want to hear about it, it'll take time, and although you might not believe it, mister, time is money to me."

I had been warned by Dulac about this very thing, so I nodded.

"That's okay."

I took from my pocket two twenty dollar bills and handed them to him. He examined the bills, heaved a great sigh that raised his belly half off his knees, then put the bills carefully away in his trousers pocket.

"And beer?"

"All the beer you want."

"A little food too?"

"Yes."

For the first time since I had been with him, his smile seemed genuine.

"Well then, mister." He paused to gulp more beer. "This is the way it was ... the Esmaldi diamonds ... it happened two years ago." He rubbed his flat, broken nose as he thought, then he went on, "I got all this dope from the cops and from my contacts ... you understand? I'm a guy with an ear to the ground. Some of it ... not much ... is guess work ... putting two and two together, but most of it is fact. It began in Miami."

Abe Schulman, so Al Barney told me, was the biggest fence in Florida. He had been in the business for some twenty years, and it was quite a business.

When the rich arrived on the Florida coast with their wives, their mistresses and their molls, their women had to be smothered in jewels – a status symbol. If you hadn't diamond necklaces, emerald and ruby brooches with ear-rings to match and jewel studded bracelets up your fat arms, you were looked upon as white trash. So the jewel thieves from all over descended on the Florida coast like a swarm of wasps, their skilful fingers collecting a harvest. But jewels were no use to them ... they wanted cash and here was where Abe Schulman came in.

He dwelt behind a glass door on which was a legend that read in tarnished gold letters:

DELANO DIAMOND MERCHANTS.
Miami – New York – Amsterdam.
President: ABE SCHULMAN.

It was true that Abe did have minor connections with Amsterdam. From time to time he made some kind of deal with certain Dutch diamond merchants: enough to justify a small income tax return and to explain why he dwelt in a tiny, shabby office on the sixteenth floor of a block overlooking Biscayne Bay.

But the real guts of his business was handling hot jewels, and in this he did extremely well, stashing away the cash – it always had to be cash – in various safe deposits in Miami, New York and Los Angeles.

When one of his contacts brought him some loot, Abe was able to say exactly how much this loot was worth. He would then pay one quarter of his evaluation. He would then remove the stones from their settings and walk the stones around to one of the many jewellers who he knew didn't ask questions and sold the stones for half their market price. In this way, working steadily now for the last twenty years, Abe had accumulated a considerable fortune: enough for him to retire on happily, but Abe just couldn't resist a bargain. He had to keep on, although he knew he was always taking a risk and the police could descend on him at any minute. But it now had become a compulsive thing with him: something he not only enjoyed, but which gave him the incentive to live.

Abe was a short, roly-poly man with hair growing out of his ears, his nose and from his shirt collar. Little clumps of black hair grew on the backs of his small, fat fingers so when he moved his hand on his desk, you had the impression of a tarantula spider coming towards you.

On a hot sunny day in May, just two years ago, Al Barney told me, Abe was sitting at his shabby desk, a dead cigar clamped between his sharp little teeth, regarding Colonel Henry Shelley with a watchful, blank expression that told anyone who knew Abe he was ready to listen, but not to believe.

Colonel Henry Shelley looked like one of those old, refined Kentucky aristocrats who own acres of land and a number of racehorses, who spend their lives either at every race meeting or sitting on their Colonial porches watching their faithful darkies doing the work. He was tall and lean with a mass of white hair, worn a little long, a straggly white moustache, a parchment yellow skin, deepset, shrewd grey eyes and a long, beaky nose. He wore a cream lightweight suit, a string tie and a ruffled shirt. His narrow trousers ended in soft Mexican boots. Looking at him, Abe had to grin with admiration. It was a beautiful performance, he told himself. He couldn't fault it. Here, before him, seemed a man of considerable substance and culture: a refined, worldly old man who anyone would be proud to entertain in their rich homes.

Colonel Henry Shelley – that, of course, wasn't his real name – was one of the smoothest and smartest con men in the business. He had spent fifteen years of his sixty-eight years behind bars. He had made a lot of money and had lost a lot of money. The names of the rich who he had swindled read like a Society Blue book. Shelley was an artist, but he was also improvident. Money slid through his old, aristocratic fingers like water.

Abe was saying, "I've got the guy you've been looking for, Henry. It's taken time. It hasn't been easy. If he doesn't satisfy you, we're in trouble. There isn't anyone I can find better."

Henry Shelley touched off the ash of his cigar into Abe's ashtray.

"You know what we want, Abe. If you think he's right, then I guess he will be right. Tell me about him."

Abe sighed.

"If you knew the trouble I've had finding him," he said. "The time I've wasted on useless punks ... the telephone calls ... "

"I can imagine. Tell me about him."

"His name is Johnny Robins," Abe said. "Good appearance. Age twenty-six. At the age of fifteen, he worked for the Rayson Lock Corporation. He worked there for five years. There is nothing he doesn't know about safes, locks and combinations." Abe jerked his thumb at the big wall safe behind him. "I thought that was pretty good, but he opened it in four minutes flat ... I timed him." Abe grinned at Shelley. "I don't keep anything in it, otherwise I wouldn't be sleeping so well. He left Rayson and became a racing driver ... he's crazy about speed. You'd better know right away that Johnny is a little tricky. He has a quick temper. There was trouble on the race track and he got fired." Abe shrugged his fat shoulders. "He busted someone's jaw ... could happen to anyone, but this guy who got busted happened to be the top shot on the track, so Johnny got the heave-ho. He then got a job at a garage, but the boss's wife got hot pants for him, so that didn't last long. The boss caught them at it and Johnny busted his nose." Abe chuckled. "Johnny sure is a mean hitter. Anyway, the boss called the cops and Johnny busted one of them before the other busted him. He spent three months in a hick jail. He told me he could have walked out any time he wanted. The locks were that simple, but he liked the company. Besides, he didn't want to embarrass the Warden who he got along with, so he stayed. Now, he is rearing to go. He's young, tough, good-looking and a beautiful baby with locks. How does it sound?"

Shelley nodded.

"Sounds right to me, Abe. You told him anything about our set-up?"

"Only that there's big money in it," Abe said, walking his fat, hairy fingers along the edge of his desk. "He's interested in big money."

"Who isn't?" Shelley stubbed out his cigar. "Well, I'd better talk to him."

"He's at the Seaview Hotel, waiting for you."

"He's registered there as Robins?"

"That's right." Abe looked up at the ceiling, then asked, "How's Martha?"

"Not as happy as she could be." Shelley took out a white silk handkerchief and touched his temples with it. It was a trick Abe admired: it showed class.

"What's biting her then?"

"She's not happy about the cut, Abe."

Abe's fat face tightened.

"She's never happy about any cut. I can't help that. Anyway, she eats too much."

"Don't change the subject, Abe." Shelley crossed one long leg over the other. "She thinks your offer of a quarter is a swindle. I'm inclined to agree with her. You see, Abe, this will be our last job. It's going to be big. The best stuff – the biggest take." He paused, then went on. "She wants to settle for a third."

"A third?" Abe managed to look shocked and amazed at the same time. "Is she crazy? I won't get a half for the stuff! What does she think I am ... the Salvation Army?"

Shelley examined his beautifully manicured fingernails, then he looked at Abe, his shrewd eyes suddenly frosty.

"If anything goes wrong, Abe, and we get the cops on our collars, we keep you out of it. You know us. We take the rap. You sit here and collect the money. Unless you do something stupid – and you won't, you're safe. Martha is sick of this racket. So am I. We want enough money to get out. A quarter won't give it to us, but a third will. That's how it is. How about it?"

Abe appeared to think. Then he shook his head, a regretful expression on his fat face.

"I can't do it, Henry. You know Martha. She's greedy. Between you and me, if I gave you a third, I'd be out of pocket. That wouldn't be fair. If I handle this stuff, I must make a reasonable profit. You understand that?"

"A third," Shelley said gently. "I know Martha too. She's set her mind on a third."

"It can't be done. Look, suppose I talk to Martha?" Abe smiled. "I can explain it to her."

"A third," Shelley repeated. "Bernie Baum is also in the market."

Abe reacted to this as if someone had driven a needle into his fat backside.

"Baum?" His voice shot up. "You haven't talked to him, have you?"

"Not yet," Shelley said quietly, "but Martha is going to if she doesn't get a third from you."

"Baum would never give her a third!"

"He might if he knew he was doing you out of a deal. Baum hates your guts, doesn't he, Abe?"

"Listen, you old swindler," Abe snarled, leaning forward and glaring at Shelley. "You don't bluff me! Baum would never give you a third ... never! I know. You don't try your con tricks on me!"

"Look, Abe," Shelley said, mildly, "don't let us argue about this. You know Martha. She wants a third. She's willing to peddle our plan around to all the big fences – and you're not the only one – until she does get a third. She will begin with Bernie. This isn't for peanuts. The take will be worth two million dollars. Even if you pick up a quarter of that, you're making nice, safe money. We want a third, Abe ... just like that or we go talk to Bernie."

Abe knew when he had struck bottom.

"That Martha!" he said in disgust. "I can't get along with women who over-eat. There's something about them ... "

"Never mind how Martha eats," Shelley said, his charming, old-world smile now in evidence. He sensed he had won. "Do we get a third or don't we?"

9

Abe glared at him.

"Yes, you do, you thief!"

"Don't get excited, Abe," Shelley said. "We're all going to make a nice slice of money. Oh, there's one other thing . . ."

Abe scowled suspiciously.

"What now?"

"Martha wants a piece of jewellery . . . a bracelet or a watch. Something fancy. This is strictly a loan, but she needs it to swing this job. You remember you promised . . ."

"There are times when I think I should have my head examined," Abe said, but he unlocked a drawer in his desk and took out a long flat jewel case. "I'm having this back, Henry . . . no tricks."

Shelley opened the case and regarded the platinum and diamond bracelet with approval.

"Don't be so suspicious, Abe. You'll end up not trusting yourself." He put the case in his pocket. "Very nice: what's it worth?"

"Eighteen thousand dollars. I want a receipt." Abe found a piece of paper, scribbled on it and pushed it across the desk. Shelley signed his name and then got to his feet.

"I'll go along and meet Johnny Robins," he said.

"I wouldn't be doing this," Abe said, staring up at him, "if Martha wasn't handling it. That tub of lard has brains."

Shelley nodded.

"Yes, she has, Abe. She has."

"I want you to understand, mister," Al Barney said to me as the barman brought his fifth refill of beer, "that I'm inclined to add a little colour to my stories. If I could spell, I'd write books myself . . . if I could write. So you'll have to go along with the poet's licence. It's just possible what I'm telling you didn't happen the way I'm telling it . . . don't get me wrong . . . I'm talking about the little details, the local colour; but when I sit here with a glass of beer in my hand, I'm inclined to let my imagination take some exercise.' He scratched his vast belly and looked at me. "That's about all the exercise I ever take."

"Go ahead," I said, "I'm still listening."

Al sipped his beer, then set the glass down on the table.

"Well, mister, we've got Abe Schulman and Henry Shelley on the stage, now we'll take a look at Martha Shelley. She and Henry hooked up after she had come out of jail. Don't imagine they were married. She knew he was one of the smoothest con men in the business and he knew she was one of the cleverest jewel thieves. But get this right – she never stole anything herself. She always organised the steals. She was so damned fat I doubt if she would be capable of stealing a dummy out of a baby's mouth, but she had a brain and Henry appreciated that. Martha had just come out of jail after a five-year stretch. Putting a woman like Martha behind bars meant she really suffered because Martha lived for food and you can imagine the kind of chow she got dished out to her in jail. She came out 80 lbs. lighter and with a vowed intention of never, repeat never, ever going back again. She met Henry at some cheap motel outside Los Angeles: a chance meeting. She knew him by reputation and he knew her by reputation. Martha had the idea on which she had been working during the time she had spent in a cell. She suddenly had the inspiration of getting Henry in on the act. He listened and fell for the idea. They decided Abe Schulman was essential to the plan if the money was to materialise and that's all they were interested in – the money. Martha had a young niece who she knew would be useful, but they would have to have another juvenile lead as well as the niece, whose name was Gilda something-or-other. Her father – Martha's brother – had been a Verdi fan: the guy who wrote operas. Gilda's old man had just come back from one of those goddam operas when the girl was born. So she got called Gilda."

"Rigoletto," I said.

Al stared at me, scratched his paunch and took another drink.

"I wouldn't know. Anyway, eventually, this girl became a trapeze artist with a small time circus. The money was no good to her and when Martha came out of jail she got the idea that she could use Gilda and Gilda liked the idea. A trapeze artist can be very useful to have around when you are working upper storey windows." Al paused and regarded his glass, then went on, "I want you to get the picture of Martha in your mind. She was about the fattest woman I've ever seen. When these old cows come down from New York, you see some fat, but Martha was in a class of her own. She was a compulsive eater . . . when she wasn't using a knife and fork, she was stuffing herself with candy and cream buns. I reckon Martha went 280 lbs. if she went a pound. She was short, square and blonde. She was around fifty-four years of age when she met up with Henry. She had more brains in her little finger than Henry had in the whole of his head. She dreamed up this big jewel take. She organised it. It was her idea that Abe should find the second juvenile lead. Abe was always in contact with the out-of-towners, and Martha was anxious the other sharks didn't hear of her idea. If they did get to hear of it, they too would have moved in.

"Martha had always been careful with her money – not like Henry, and she had undertaken to finance the operation. She didn't tell Henry how much capital she had. In actual fact, she had around twelve thousand dollars tucked up her girdle and she had made up her mind to put the operation on as it should be put on.

"She took a three-room suite at the Plaza Hotel on Bay-Shore Drive. Nothing over luxe, but good. She got the penthouse suite which suited Gilda who believed in having comfort for nothing. It pleased Henry too who liked to live up to his phony back-ground, and besides, it wasn't costing him anything either.

"While Henry was talking to Abe, Martha was sitting

under a sun umbrella on the private terrace that went with the pent-house, eating peppermint creams while Gilda was lying in the full sun on a Li-Lo as naked as the back of my hand ... "

Martha Shelley, better known in the underworld as Fats Gummrich, put two fat fingers into the carton and selected a chocolate which she regarded with affection before popping it into her mouth.

"Cover yourself up, girl," she said, looking at Gilda's naked brown back. "Henry could walk in at any moment ... what would he think?"

Gilda, lying face down, rested her head on her crossed arms, lifted her long, lovely-looking legs and tightened her lean buttocks. She giggled.

"I know what he would think," she said. "But who cares? That old goat's got beyond it."

"No man ever gets beyond it – anyway, not in his mind," Martha said. "Put something on!"

Gilda turned on her back, crossing her legs, and looked up at the brilliant blue sky through her sun goggles.

She was twenty-five years of age: her hair was thick, worn long and the colour of a ripe chestnut. She had large green eyes, fringed by long, dark lashes and one of those gamin, interesting faces that make men's heads turn – not strictly beautiful, but beautiful enough. Her sun-tanned body was sensational. There was no bikini whiteness. When Gilda sunbathed, she sunbathed in the nude.

"You eat too much," she said, lifting her cone-shaped breasts. "How can you go on stuffing yourself hour after hour ... ugh!"

"I'm not talking about me, I'm talking about you!" Martha snapped. "Cover yourself up! I don't want Henry to get upset. He has old-fashioned ideas."

Gilda waved her long legs in the air as she gave a hoot of laughter.

"That's funny! The old buzzard gave me the biggest

bruise on my bottom I've had in weeks! Look . . . " She rolled over, pointing.

Martha controlled a snigger.

"Well, maybe he isn't all that old-fashioned, but cover yourself up, honey. I've enough trouble without Henry getting out of hand."

Grimacing, Gilda pulled a wrap off a chair by her.

"What trouble? I thought everything was fixed." She laid the wrap across her middle.

"Do you want one of these?" Martha held up a peppermint cream.

"In this heat? No, thank you!" Gilda turned on her side to stare up at the massive woman under the sun umbrella. "What trouble?"

"No trouble," Henry Shelley said coming silently out on to the terrace. He eyed Gilda's exposed breasts with appreciation. "No trouble at all. Abe has everything taken care of." He watched with regret Gilda pull the wrap up to her chin.

"Take your eyes off me, you old lecher!" she said.

"Well, they do say a priest is allowed to read a menu in Lent," Henry said with a sly grin and sat down near Martha.

"That's enough of that!" Martha said sharply. "What did Abe say?"

"Well, as was expected, he screamed to high heaven, but he promised in the end to pay a third. He's found us a good boy. He'll be along in a couple of days. He's getting fitted for his uniform and he is buying a car . . . he knows about cars. In a couple of days' time, we can get moving."

"You've seen him?"

Henry nodded. He touched his temples with his silk handkerchief while he eyed Gilda's exposed legs. Pretty girl, he thought a little sadly. In his past, he had had much amusement with pretty girls.

"He's made to measure. A little tough, but we'll be able to work with him, I'm sure."

"What do you mean – tough?" Martha asked, delving into the carton again.

"He has a quick temper. He's inclined to hit out if someone doesn't please him, but I know that type. He'll be all right in any emergency." The old grey eyes moved from Gilda to Martha. The movement of his eyes alerted Martha. She looked at Gilda. "Suppose you get dressed, honey? I thought we would all go down to the Casino."

"That means you two old squares want to yak together," Gilda said. She got to her feet, holding the wrap against her and then walked across the terrace, swinging her naked hips while Henry watched, entranced.

"Lovely girl," he murmured, pulling at his moustache.

"Wants her bottom smacked!" Martha said, outraged. "What about this boy?"

Henry explained what Abe had told him, then went on, "I met him and I like him. There's no doubt he can handle this job. It's just ... " He fingered his string tie. "There's Gilda ... "

"You mean he could fall for her?"

"He'll do that for sure."

"Well, so what?" Martha dug out another chocolate. "She needs a man. I'd rather it be someone in the family ... that wouldn't worry me. Can he handle safes?"

"Abe swears by him."

"Did you get a brooch or something from Abe?"

Henry took from his pocket the jewel case.

"Abe extended himself. It's worth eighteen grand."

Martha examined the bracelet, then nodded her approval.

"Do you think we are going to have trouble with Abe, Henry?"

"I don't think so. He's tricky, but he's co-operating all along the line. The big test is when we get the stuff and ask for the money."

Martha brooded for a long moment, then she slipped the jewel case into her handbag, lying on the table.

"Do you think it is going to work, Henry?" she asked, suddenly a little doubtful.

Henry crossed his long legs and stared out at the busy harbour below.

"It's got to work, hasn't it?" he said.

Two days later, the three were on the terrace: none of them revealing the slight tension they were all feeling. Martha and Henry sat in lounging chairs under the shade of the big sun umbrella. Gilda, in a white skimpy bikini that set off her golden skin, lay in the full sun.

Martha was working on a piece of embroidery, stretched on a frame and from time to time, dipping into a big box of chocolates Henry had bought at the gift shop down in the lobby. Henry was studying the Stock Exchange column in the *New York Times*. In his imagination, he bought and sold many stocks and could spend hours working out his imaginary profits. Gilda lay limply on the Li-Lo, feeling the rays of the sun burning into her. She could lie that way for hours. Neither Martha nor Henry had an idea what went on in her mind while she sunbathed. Henry thought probably nothing, but Martha, who knew her better, wasn't so sure.

The sound of the telephone brought them alert. Martha put down her embroidery frame. Gilda lifted her head. Henry dropped his newspaper, got to his feet and walked with that slow gait that reminded Martha of the uneven movements of a stork into the living-room.

They heard him say "Yes?" in that deep aristocratic voice of his, then, "Tell him to come up if you please."

Henry returned to the terrace.

"Our chauffeur has arrived."

"Cover yourself up, Gilda!" Martha said. "Put that wrap on!"

"Oh, for God's sake!" Gilda exclaimed impatiently, but she got up and pulled on the wrap. She walked over to the balcony rail and leaned over it, staring down at the crowded swimming pool in the hotel garden.

Johnny Robins made an impact on Martha. He came on to the terrace, immaculate in a well-cut, dark blue chauffeur's uniform, a peaked cap under his arm. He was a tall, powerfully built man with close-cut black hair, a narrow forehead, a blunt nose, eyes set wide apart and hazel-green, and a thin, tight mouth. Everything about him hinted of strength with a hidden vein of violence. He walked like a professional fighter: relaxed, and with silent, springy steps.

"Hello, Johnny," Martha said as she eyed him. "Welcome."

"Hello. I've heard about you," Johnny said, and his hard face lit up with an easy smile. "The old gentleman has been telling me about you."

"Don't call me that!" Henry said curtly, annoyed. "You call me the Colonel!"

Johnny threw back his head and laughed.

"Sure ... why not?" His eyes went from Martha to Gilda's shapely back. Even the wrap couldn't disguise Gilda's contours. Watching him, the other two saw the look of awakening interest. "Is that Miss Rigoletto I've been hearing about?"

Gilda turned slowly and surveyed him from head to foot. She felt a stab of excitement run through her at the sight of this man, but her expression remained remote and disinterested.

They regarded each other, then Johnny stroked the side of his jaw with his thumb.

"Ah ... hmmm." He turned to Martha. "I think I'm going to like it here." He grinned and began to unbutton his double-breasted jacket. "Phew! I'm hot. Have you seen the beauty I've bought you? Look at it. The steel grey job on the drive-in."

Martha hauled herself to her feet. She and Henry joined Gilda at the balcony rail. They all looked down at the Cadillac Fleetwood Brougham parked by the entrance to the hotel.

Martha sucked in her breath. "Hell! What did that cost me?" she demanded, turning to glare at Johnny.

"Two thousand eight hundred dollars," he told her. "It's a giveaway price. I'll sell it again for four thousand. You can't lose."

Martha peered down at the car again. She felt a tingle of excitement run up her larded spine. This was a car! This was the kind of car she had often dreamed about when shut in her cell.

"You're sure? You really mean you can sell it again for four?"

Johnny squinted at her: his eyes turned hard.

"When I say something, I say something."

Martha studied him, then she nodded, satisfied. Abe, she felt, had made the right choice. This man might be difficult, but she was now sure that he was right for the job, and that was all Martha cared about.

"Would you like a drink, Johnny?"

He shook his head.

"I don't drink." He took off his jacket and hung it over the back of one of the chairs, then he sat down.

"Let's talk business. The old ... the Colonel gave me the general outline. Now I want details."

Martha lowered her enormous bulk into a chair near his. She relaxed back, her fingers hunting for a chocolate. Henry took a chair near hers. Gilda pulled her wrap closer and more provocatively around her and remained by the balcony rail.

Johnny looked at her.

"Isn't Miss Rigoletto in on this?" he asked.

"Of course ... come and sit down, Gilda," Martha said, patting a chair near hers.

"You yak ... I'm taking a swim," Gilda said, and without looking at Johnny, she left the terrace.

Al Barney finished the last of his beer, then rattled the glass impatiently on the table until the barman brought him a refill.

"All this talking makes me thirsty," he said, catching my eye. "I get scratchy at the back of my throat."

I said I understood.

"Well, mister, I now want to fill you in how Martha got her idea for this big steal," Al said after a long gulp of beer. "Around eight years ago, she was running a little gang of smart jewel thieves – three of them. They did a hold-up job – a little crude. There was a rich old cow loaded with jewels who went every night always at the same time to the Miami Casino. Martha just couldn't resist the temptation. She organised the stick-up. The guys got the loot, then Martha was hit by a hurricane. What she didn't know was the jewels were insured by the National Fidelity of California, and that is the toughest, roughest insurance company in the whole of the States. They have a man there named Maddox who looks after the Claims Department. To him, so I'm told, paying out a claim is like losing a quart of his own blood. Tangling with Maddox is about ten times as dangerous as tangling with a puff adder.

"One of the stick-up artists had a missing finger, and in spite of being scared half-dotty, the victim of the hold-up noticed this. Maddox had the most comprehensive card index of every jewel thief in the world: big and little. He had only to press a few buttons and out came Joe Salik's card. It took Maddox's investigators three days to pick up Joe and then they worked him over – make no mistake about this. Maddox's investigators play rough. Joe talked, and Martha found herself behind bars.

"She shared her cell with a middle-aged woman who was in for embezzlement, and this woman, her name was Hetty something-or-other, was a talker. She had worked for Alan Frisby, an insurance broker in Paradise City. He acted for all the top insurance companies in the country. If you wanted to insure something special, you went along and talked to Frisby and he told you impartially which company to go to for your particular coverage, the best rates and he fixed the deal. He had a very sound, flourishing business.

"Well, Hetty talked, and Martha listened and from what she got told, she realised how she could organise the big steal. She got from Hetty inside information that nobody should know, and it was this information that inspired Martha to make the plan that she hoped would put her on easy street for the rest of her eating life." Al paused, shifted his enormous body to a more comfortable position, then asked, "You're following so far, mister?"

I said I was.

The Villa Bellevue was on Lansdown Avenue: one of the swank avenues of Paradise City. It was a compact, de luxe, ranch house type of building with four bedrooms, four bathrooms, an enormous living-room, a de luxe kitchen, servants' quarters, a big terrace and a garage for four cars. Leading down by steps from the terrace was a small, screened private beach, equipped with hot and cold showers, changing rooms and a cocktail bar. The ranch house was owned by Jack Carson, a wealthy New York stockbroker who had bought the place as an investment. He rented it furnished for $1,500 a month. After some heavy haggling, Martha got it for $1,300 and signed up for three months. The price outraged her, but she knew that if she was going to swing this job she had to have the right back-ground and the right address.

A day after Johnny had joined the trio, the Cadillac moved off from the Plaza Hotel, heading for Paradise City. Johnny, in his uniform, was at the wheel. Next to him was Flo, the coloured maid, who had been with Martha now for the past three years.

Flo was a tall, thin Negress who, at one time, had been a skilful shoplifter, but eventually the cops caught up with her and, like Martha, she had decided she would never go back behind the bars again. She and Martha got along well together. Flo never asked questions. She guessed there was some job on, but she didn't want to know about it. Her job was to supply Martha and the rest of them with meals, keep the villa clean and pick up $100 a week which was what Martha was paying her.

In the back of the roomy Cadillac were Martha, Henry and Gilda.

During the twenty-four hours that they remained at the Plaza Hotel while waiting to move to paradise City, Gilda and Johnny probed each other out: like a dog and a bitch, not quite knowing if they would fight or make love.

There was nothing that Gilda didn't know about men. She had had her first sexual experience at the age of fifteen. She liked sex, and had had many men during the following years, but now, at the age of twenty-five, she had decided she wanted to get married and to settle down. This job that Martha was planning would give her, she hoped, the necessary capital to have a home, possibly a husband and possibly a family.

Johnny interested her. She knew from long experience that he wanted her the moment he set eyes on her. She knew too that having Johnny as a lover would be one of the most exciting of all her sexual experiences. She liked the look of him: he could just possibly be the partner she had been hoping to find ... just possibly. She wanted to get to know him better, so she told herself to play it cool. No matter how much he put on the pressure, he wasn't going to have her. No ring – no bed. If, eventually, there was no ring ... then it would be just too bad.

They arrived at the villa late in the afternoon. They were all impressed with it.

"I'll say!" Martha exclaimed, heaving her bulk from room to room, inspecting everything. "So it should be good! Look what I'm paying ... thirteen hundred dollars a month!"

She chose the largest and best bedroom for herself, gave the second best to Henry and the other two bedrooms which were pleasant enough to Gilda and Johnny: all rooms had a view over the beach and the sea.

Gilda went immediately to her room, changed into a bikini and then ran down the steps to the sea. A few minutes later, Johnny joined her. Stripped down to brief trunks, his muscular, powerful lean body was impressive. Seeing him as he came running across the sand, Gilda again felt a stab of almost pain run through her. To be made love to by a man like this! She forced herself to turn away and she swam with powerful, professional strokes out to sea. She prided herself on her prowess as an expert swimmer and she was confident that she would not only impress him, but leave him far behind. It came as a distinct shock when she paused to find him just behind her. She shook the water out of her eyes and lifted her eyebrows.

"You're quite a swimmer," she said, treading water.

"You're not so bad either." He grinned. "Race you back?"

She nodded.

Martha, sitting on the terrace, holding a carton of chocolates and dipping into it from time to time with Henry by her side, watched the two as they raced back to the shore.

"She's showing off," she said as she saw Gilda was leaving Johnny behind.

Henry watched with critical interest.

"Women show off to men ... men to women ... that's nature."

Johnny just got ahead in the last twenty yards, but only just. There wasn't more than inches between them as he was the first to touch the sea wall.

"Women!" Henry shook his head. "Wonderful creatures. She could have beaten him by ten yards. Did you see she deliberately slowed down to let him win?"

Martha snorted.

"Well, if it makes him happy ..."

"Of course it does." Henry crossed one stork-like leg over the other. "Men never like being beaten by women."

CHAPTER TWO

Alan Frisby laid down a file he was studying and looked inquiringly at his secretary as she came into his office.

"Colonel and Mrs Shelley are here," she told him. "They have an appointment."

"Sure ... send them right in." Frisby pushed aside the file and leaned back in his executive's chair. He was a slim, tall man who had been in the insurance business longer than he cared to remember. Now, at the age of fifty-five, with a first-class business under his control, he was hoping very soon that his son who was at the University would qualify and then take over some of the harder work.

He was a little startled when Martha came into his office which until her appearance had semed to him to be large, but now as she moved towards him, the room seemed to shrink by her enormous size. The tall, stork-like man who followed her was obviously Colonel Shelley, her husband.

Frisby got to his feet, shook hands and arranged chairs. Martha sat down, but Henry moved to the window, pulling at his moustache and Frisby got the impression that the Colonel was being petulant for some reason or other.

Seeing him looking at Henry, Martha leaned forward and patted his arm with her hot, fat hand.

"Take no notice of the Colonel, Mr Frisby," she said. "You have no idea the trouble I had getting him here ... he just doesn't believe in insurance."

"Never have done ... never will do," Henry growled as he moved around the office. "Waste of money. You lose something, and it's your own damned fault. The thing to do is not to lose anything!"

Frisby had dealt with all kinds of eccentrics. After giving the Colonel his professional, understanding smile which was returned by a stony stare, he turned his attention to Martha.

"This is really nothing much, Mr Frisby," Martha said. "The dear Colonel has just bought me a present for our wedding anniversary and I want it insured."

"Damn nonsense," Henry said from behind Frisby. "If you lose it, you deserve to lose it!"

"Don't pay any attention to him," Martha said, smiling. "The Colonel has ideas of his own . . . I have ideas of my own. I think I should insure my present." With a little flourish, she put the jewel case on Frisby's desk. "After all, he paid eighteen thousand dollars for it . . . you never know . . . it could be stolen."

As Frisby picked up the case, Henry, a small piece of putty in his lean old hand, pressed the putty against the lock of the big filing cabinet that stood behind Frisby. The movement was swift, and immediately Henry came around Frisby's desk and walked over to the window. He put the impression in a small tin box he had brought with him and dropped the box into his pocket.

"This is beautiful," Frisby said, admiring the bracelet. "I can arrange to have it covered. You should have it insured."

"I deal with the Los Angeles & California," Martha said. "They take care of my other jewels."

"That's fine, Mrs Shelley. I work with L.A. & C. I can fix it. I take it you want it covered for a year?"

Martha nodded.

"Yes . . . I would like that.'

Frisby checked his rates book.

"Thirty dollars, Mrs Shelley . . . that gives you full coverage."

"We'll settle right now. Henry, have you thirty dollars?"

"I have thirty dollars," Henry said, scowling. "Throwing good money away." But he drew a thick roll from his hip pocket, peeled off three $10 bills and dropped them on the desk.

"Where are you staying, Mrs Shelley?" Frisby asked as he made out a receipt.

"Bellevue on Lansdown Avenue."

Frisby looked impressed.

"That's Jack Carson's place?"

"That's right. I've rented it for three months."

"Would you have your policy number?"

"No, but you can check with them. It's Colonel Henry Shelley, 1247 Hill Crescent, Los Angeles."

Frisby made a note, then seeing Henry was peering at the photo-copying machine on a stand by the window, he said, "Are you interested in these machines, Colonel?"

Henry turned.

"Don't understand them. Glad I've got out of business. Too damned old now to cope with anything."

"Now that will do," Martha said, putting the jewel case into her handbag. "You're not all that old." She heaved herself to her feet.

When they had gone, Frisby called the Los Angeles & Californian Insurance Corporation. He always checked on strangers as Martha knew he would. He was told that Colonel Shelley was a recent client of theirs. His wife's jewellery was covered for $150,000. He wasn't to know, nor the Insurance Company, that Abe had loaned the jewels to Martha to get them insured. Nor were they to know that 1247 Hill Crescent was merely an accommodation address, owned by Abe, and used by any number of jewel thieves who needed a respectable background.

Martha climbed heavily into the Cadillac, parked outside Frisby's office block. Henry followed her in.

Johnny set the Cadillac in motion.

"Well?"

"Looks simple," Henry reported. "No alarms. Doors to the office easy. The only tricky one is the lock on the filing cabinet, but I have an impression that might give you a lead."

"How about the janitor?"

"He looks the kind of slob who does as little as possible."

Johnny grunted.

"We could be in there a couple of hours. The best time would be at eight o'clock. We can't work in the dark."

"Yes." Henry gnawed at his moustache. "The business district is deserted by eight. You'll have a full hour and a half before it gets dark."

When they reached the villa, they had a conference.

Martha explained the operation.

"I got this dope from a woman who worked for Frisby," she said, peering into the depleted box of chocolates. "What I want are Frisby's insurance records for jewellery. This woman told me Frisby keeps a complete file in the cabinet in his office. It should be easy to find. It had a tab on it marked 'Local Jewellery Coverage'. In front of the file is a list of names and addresses, values and details of where the jewels are stored – whether in a safe at home or in a bank or what-have-you. This I want. With this list, we'll know exactly what is worth going after and how tricky it will be to get at. Without the list, we'll just waste time and get nowhere. There is a photo-copying machine in the office. All you have to do is to photo-copy the records, put the originals back in the cabinet as you found them, relock the cabinet and we will be in business."

"The machine is a Zennox," Henry said to Gilda. "The directions are printed on the lid. The machine is loaded. with paper. All you have to do is to put the originals on the machine and press a button."

Gilda nodded.

Henry took the tin box from his pocket and handed it to Johnny.

"That's the impression of the cabinet lock. Tell you anything?"

Johnny opened the box and examined the impression. He grimaced.

"It tells me a lot. This is a Herman lock and they are damned tricky." He sat back, staring out at the sea while he thought.

Martha, a large cream filled chocolate held in her fingers, watched him, suddenly alarmed.

"Can't you handle it?" she demanded, her voice a little shrill. "Abe said you could handle any lock!"

Johnny turned his head slowly. His cold eyes surveyed her.

"Don't panic, Fats," he said. "I can handle any lock, but I want to give it a little thought."

Gilda giggled.

"Don't call me Fats!" Martha snarled, outraged. "Now, listen to me ... "

"Screw you," Johnny said. "Let me think, will you?"

Henry stroked his moustache and looked at Gilda. His heavy tortoise-like eyelid lowered a trifle. Martha was so shaken she put the chocolate back in the box, but she kept quiet.

Finally, Johnny nodded.

"It can be done. I'll have to go to Miami for some key blanks. It would be too risky to get them here. Yes, okay, it can be done."

Martha drew in a long, deep breath that lifted her enormous bosom.

"You had me scared for a moment. Everything depends on getting those records."

Johnny looked away from her. He made no attempt to conceal his impatience with her; nor his dislike.

"We'll need another car," he said. "The Caddy is fine for a front, but it gets noticed. I'll rent a Hertz." He got to his feet and went into the living-room. The three heard him calling Hertz.

"Hello, Fats," Gilda said and gave a hoot of laughter. "I wish you could have seen your face! Oh, boy! Did you have to take it!"

"Shut up, you little bitch!" Martha snarled. "I know you've got hot pants for him! You ... "

"Ladies!" Henry broke in sharply. "That will do! We're working together, and we are in business together."

Gilda got up from her chair. She looked at Martha who was glaring at her, then she made a cheeky face and walked off the terrace, swinging her hips.

Johnny came back.

"That's fixed. I'm picking the car up at the office. Well, I'll get off. I'll be back around eight o'clock."

"Wait a moment, Johnny," Henry said, "as you're going to Miami would you take the bracelet back to Abe? I bet he's laying an egg wondering what has happened to it. Give it to him, Martha."

Martha hesitated, then handed the jewel case to Johnny.

"Don't lose it."

Johnny grinned at her.

"Think I'm going to run off with it?"

"I said don't lose it!" Martha snapped.

When he had gone, Henry lit a cigar and stretched out his long legs with a sigh of content.

"Abe picked the right one, Martha," he said. "He's a professional."

"Fats!" Martha muttered. "I'll remember that!"

She was about to take another chocolate, then suddenly she pushed the box violently away from her and glared out to sea.

Henry hid a grin.

Johnny returned around eight-thirty. He had seen Abe and given back the bracelet and collected Henry's receipt. He had also the key blanks which he had got through a friend of Abe's and also the necessary tools to do the job. He said he would work on the key in the morning.

Flo gave them lobster thermidor for dinner and after Martha had eaten her way through two large lobsters and a pint of ice cream, they settled down for the evening.

Gilda was a TV addict. She turned on the set and anchored herself to it. Henry, with pad and pencil, sat with Martha on the terrace while he worked out his imaginary profit and loss on the Stock Exchange. Martha stitched away at her embroidery. Johnny sat away from them, looking down at the lighted harbour, watching the yachts and the headlights of the cars making a continuous double ribbon of light as the cars crawled around the bay.

At eleven-thirty, Martha hoisted herself to her feet.

"I'm going to bed," she announced.

No one bothered to say anything and she plodded past Gilda, who was staring, hypnotised by the lighted screen, snorted and then made her way to the kitchen. She looked hopefully into the refrigerator. Flo always left a selection of cold food waiting for her. For some moments, Martha hesitated between a breast of chicken or a fillet of fried sole. She decided on the chicken and putting it on a paper plate – a stack of them always stood on the top of the refrigerator – she went to bed.

Twenty minutes later, Henry completed his balance sheet. He was delighted to find that he was ahead. He folded the newspaper and said, "Good night, all," and went to bed.

Gilda felt a quickening of her blood as she heard Henry's bedroom door close. The play she was watching was pure corn. She looked through the open doors, leading on to the terrace. Johnny was sitting there, his feet on the iron rail, motionless, looking down at the scene below. She got to her feet, turned off the set and wandered out on to the terrace. She was wearing white stretch pants and a red halter. Her chestnut coloured hair was free about her shoulders. She was aware that she looked very attractive and this feeling gave her confidence. She came to stand near Johnny. She put her arms on the rail and peered down at the distant harbour. Johnny made no move to show he had noticed her. She waited for a long moment, then said, "What are you going to do with the money when you get it?"

"I haven't got it yet."

"Assume you will ... what will you do with it?"

He looked up at her.

"Why do you want to know?"

She turned.

"Because I'm interested."

"Well, if you're that interested, I'll tell you." He took a pack of cigarettes from his pocket. "Want one?"

"No, thanks."

"I'm going to buy a garage." He lit the cigarette and blew smoke towards the star-studded sky. "I have one lined up. It handles fast cars ... specialises. It's not doing much now, but then the guy who owns it doesn't really understand fast cars ... I do. I could make a big thing out of it."

She felt a little pang of jealousy. Men always had some project in mind ... a garage, for God's sake!

"Where is it?" she asked, forcing herself to show interest.

"A little place called Carmel on the Pacific Coast."

She was aware of a dreamy note in his voice and this irritated her.

"Well, don't count on it ... we may not get the money," she said sourly.

"It's worth a try."

There was a long pause, then as he was now staring down at the harbour again, she spoke sharply, "Obviously you're not interested in what I would do with my share, are you?"

Johnny flicked ash over the rail.

"Not particularly. You'll spend it ... women always spend money."

"I suppose they do." She felt an urge to touch him, but she restrained herself.

Johnny suddenly looked directly at her. His eyes went from her head to her feet and then up again.

Gilda felt her nipples harden under that look. She tried to out-stare him, but she failed. She looked away.

"Do you want to come to bed with me now?" he asked.

She wanted to cry out: "Of course! Why do you sit there like a goddamn, superior dummy? Why don't you grab me ... I'm here to be grabbed!"

Her voice shaking with frustration and anger, she said aloud, "Is that what you say to every girl you meet?"

He grinned, his eyes moving over her.

"It saves time, doesn't it? Do you or don't you?"

"No, I don't!" Gilda said furiously and she walked off the terrace. She heard him mutter something and she paused, turned and demanded, "What did you say?"

"I said who are you kidding?" Johnny repeated and laughed.

"Oh! I hate you!"

"The same old corny dialogue. You watch TV too much."

She ran to her bedroom and slammed the door.

The following night, soon after ten-thirty, the tension between Martha and Henry became electric. They were sitting on the terrace, waiting. Henry was smoking a cigar too fast so that it burned unevenly. Martha gnawed at a turkey leg, every now and then laying it down to wipe her fingers on a Kleenex and then picking it up again.

"Don't keep looking at your watch," Henry said sharply, having just looked at his own. "It's getting on my nerves!"

"On *your* nerves? What about *mine*?"

"All right, Martha, don't let's get panicky." Henry was making a strenuous effort to control his own fluttering nerves. "They've only been gone two and a half hours."

"Do you think the cops have got them?" Martha asked, leaning forward and waving the turkey leg. "That Johnny! I'm scared of him. He could talk. He doesn't like me."

31

Henry looked with disgust at his unevenly burning cigar and crushed it out in the big glass ashtray.

"You're working yourself up for nothing," he said, trying to control the little shake in his voice. "He could have had trouble with that lock."

"But Abe said he could handle any lock!"

"Well, you know Abe ... "

Martha bit into the succulent dark flesh of the turkey leg and munched, staring down at the lights below.

"I can't go back to prison, Henry," she said finally. "That's something I can't do. I'll take an overdose."

"There's no need to talk like that." Henry paused and thought back on those fifteen years he had spent in a cell: an experience he too was determined not to repeat. An overdose? Well, why not? He was sixty-eight. There were times when he thought of death with pleasure. He knew he was walking a tightrope. If it hadn't been for Martha, God knows what he would be doing now ... certainly not sitting on this terrace with this view, after an excellent dinner and a good brandy to hand. This would be his last steal. It was, he knew, a gamble. He was healthy enough. There was nothing wrong with him. If he got the money and avoided the police, he could settle in a two-room apartment in Nice, France. He had done some clever and profitable jobs in and around Monte Carlo in his younger days. He had always planned to retire to Nice. But if the job went wrong – and it could – then it would be better to finish his life. With his record and with the size of the job against him, he would go away for at least ten years. That meant he would die in a cell. Martha was no fool. She was right. An overdose would be the best way out.

"But I am talking like that," Martha went on. "They'll never get me alive."

"This is going to be all right, Martha. You're getting worked up." Henry wished he believed what he was saying. He paused, then took from his leather case another cigar which he lit carefully. "Have you a pill or something?"

She looked at him and nodded.

"Yes."

Henry crossed one long leg over the other, hesitated, then asked, "One to spare?"

"Yes, Henry."

"We won't need them, but a sword is better than a stick in any fight."

Gilda and Johnny came out on to the terrace. Neither of the two had heard them arrive. They both stiffened, turned and looked expectantly.

Gilda dropped into a chair. She lifted her hair off her shoulders with a little shuddering movement. Johnny came over to Martha.

"Here it is," he said and put on the table four sheets of photo-copy paper. "It wasn't easy."

Martha dropped the half-eaten turkey leg back on the paper plate. She looked up at Johnny's hard, expressionless face.

"Any trouble?"

"Here and there . . . nothing we couldn't handle. The janitor wasn't such a slob. He nearly caught us, but not quite. Anyway, we've done it, and there it is!"

"You really mean there's going to be no trouble?" Martha demanded.

"He was marvellous!" Gilda said huskily. "He unlocked all the locks and relocked them. He had to spend eighty minutes getting that filing cabinet open and I nearly walked up the wall! But he didn't! And when we got the file and photo-copied it, he spent another half-hour relocking the file cabinet."

"Be quiet!" Johnny said. "It was a job . . . it's been done. I'm going for a swim."

He left them and ran down the steps to the beach below.

"I told you, Martha," Henry said. "He is a good man."

"You don't know how good," Gilda said. "It was magic. The way he opened the doors . . . the way he knelt for all

33

that time fiddling with that cabinet lock, talking to it as if he was making love to a woman; so gently, so ... I've never watched anything like it, and when the lock yielded as a woman might have yielded, he gave a moaning sound that ... well, you know ... " Gilda stopped short, her face flushing, and she got to her feet.

"Have a drink," Henry said gently. "Let me get you something."

Gilda didn't hear him. She went to the balcony rail and leaning over, she watched Johnny as he swam far out to sea.

The other two looked at each other, then Martha wiped her fingers on the Kleenex and picked up the photo-copies.

The tension of breaking into the office block, the moment when they had nearly run into the janitor who was wandering around on the second floor landing, the long wait while Johnny had fought with the lock, the final triumph had now left Gilda limp and exhausted.

Leaving the other two examining the photo-copies, she went into her bedroom, stripped off and took a cold shower. It was a hot night with a brilliant moon. The windows were wide open, but the room still felt close. She lay naked on the bed, staring out at the moon, her ankles crossed, her hands behind her head. She lay like that for a long time, her mind reliving her experience, reliving the jolt of terror as Johnny grabbed her and pulled her back into the shadows as the shambling figure of the janitor had passed them.

She was vaguely aware of the light on the terrace being turned off and Martha stumping off to the refrigerator. She heard Henry's door close.

She wondered what Johnny was doing. If he came now to her room, she wouldn't have refused him. Her body ached for him. She wanted him as she had never wanted any other man.

But Johnny didn't come.

*

34

At exactly eight-thirty a.m., Flo wheeled the breakfast-trolley into Martha's bedroom. She was surprised to find Martha already out of bed, sitting on her small terrace, busily scribbling with a pencil on a sheet of paper.

"Mornin', Miss Martha ... you all right?" Flo asked, her big, black eyes rolling.

"Of course I'm all right, you fool!" Martha snapped. She laid down her pencil.

She regarded the trolley with greedy eyes. Flo always provided something exciting for breakfast and always served it well.

"Tell the Colonel I want to talk to him in an hour. Where is he?"

"Taking coffee on the terrace below, Miss Martha."

"Well, tell him."

Half an hour later, Martha had demolished four pancakes and syrup, four lambs' kidneys with creamed potatoes, five slices of toast with cherry jam and three cups of coffee. She pushed aside the trolley and leaned back in her chair with a sigh of content as there came a knock on the door.

Henry came in, looking like a lean old stork, a lighted cigar between his fingers.

"Sit down," Martha said. "Do you want some coffee? There's some left."

"No, thank you, I've had my coffee." Henry sat down and crossed his legs. "Well?"

"I've made a list ... take a look at it." Martha gave him the sheet of paper she had been working on.

Henry studied the list, stroking his moustache, then he nodded.

"I also made a list ... we're thinking along the same lines, but you've left out the Esmaldi diamonds. What's wrong with them?"

Martha shook her head. She made a face as if she had bitten into a quince.

"Do you mean to tell me, Henry, that you would be

stupid enough to go after the Esmaldi diamonds?" she demanded.

Henry stared at her.

"I don't see why not. They're worth $350,000. Abe would go mad with joy to have them. So why not?"

"Abe isn't going mad with joy, and I'll tell you for why. The Esmaldi diamonds are insured with the National Fidelity, and that means Maddox. That sonofabitch put me away for five years! He's the smartest and most dangerous bastard in the insurance racket. I've made certain that all this stuff we are going after isn't covered by the National Fidelity. The other insurance punks are not in the same class as Maddox. I've tangled with him once – never again!"

Henry nodded.

"I didn't know."

"Well, you know now." Martha gathered her wrap around her. "Where's Johnny?"

"On the terrace."

She heaved herself to her feet and went to the balcony rail. She bawled down to Johnny to come up.

She returned to her chair, eyed the depleted breakfast-trolley, then seeing a slice of currant loaf still on the bread plate, she buttered it heavily and began to eat it.

Johnny came out on to her terrace.

"Sit down," Martha said. "We're now in business." She paused to wipe her mouth with a paper napkin. "We have a short list of people who own a whale of a lot of expensive jewellery which is kept in their homes in Raysons' safes. The collection is worth $1,800,000. Take a third of that which is what that thief Abe Schulman will pay and we get net $600,000. The way I split it up is that you get $125,000. How do you like that?"

Johnny studied her, his face expressionless.

"Sounds okay. I'll believe it when I get it," he said finally.

"That's right." Martha nodded. "Well now, Abe tells me you can handle safes and locks. I've selected the people who keep their jewels in Raysons' safes because I understand you've worked for Raysons. How about it, Johnny?"

Johnny lit a cigarette, slowly and deliberately, while he stared at Martha, then he said, "Let me tell you about Raysons' safes. They are very special. For one thing they can't be broken open. For another, for the owner of the safe, they are absolutely fool-proof. Anyone crazy enough to try to break into one of these safes is asking for a long stretch in jail."

Martha stiffened, then leaned forward, her little eyes flinty, her face a granite mask.

"Are you telling me you can't open a goddamn Raysons' safe?" she shrilled, blood rushing into her face.

"Oh, take it easy," Johnny said, his expression bored. "The way you eat and act, you'll be dead in a year. Don't yell at me!"

"God!" Martha screamed, beating her fat fists on the arms of the chair. "I won't take talk like that from you, you goddamn ... "

"Shut up!" Johnny snarled and leaned forward. "Hear me? Shut your fat mouth!"

Henry watched all this, smoking his cigar, his legs crossed, his expression interested.

"Are you telling me to shut up? *You?*" Martha bawled.

Johnny got to his feet.

"No, I'm not telling you to shut up. I made a mistake. Yell as much as you want to. I don't work with people like you. Find someone else. Someone who knows how to open a Rayson." He started across the terrace.

Martha shouted, "Johnny! Come back! I'm sorry!"

Johnny paused, turned and then grinned. He returned to his chair and sat down.

"Forget it. I guess we're both a little temperamental." He paused to light a cigarette, then went on, "Let me tell you more about the Raysons' safes ... let me explain their system. Take anyone who has a lot of money, a lot of jewels, bonds." He paused to look at Martha. "Have you cooled down? Are you listening?"

"I'm listening," Martha said, struggling with her temper. "Go on!"

"Well, this somebody wants to stash away his valuables. So he goes to Raysons and tells them his problem. To Raysons it is no problem. They have heard it all before. You want a foolproof safe, sir – we have it. You have to expect a hole knocked in your wall to take the safe, but Raysons do the whole job ... no fuss ... just one hundred per cent efficiency. Now a Raysons' safe is a fireproof, foolproof, burglar-proof box with a sliding door that is controlled by a patent electronic gimmick that opens and shuts the door by pressing a button. There are two controls. Each control is hidden somewhere in the room or even out of the room, depending on what the customers want. Only the owner of the safe, Raysons and the man who fits the safe know where the controls are hidden. The man who fits the safe has been working for them for years and he gets a big wage. He can't be got at. He's that type of man. The controls are about the size of a pinhead and can be concealed anywhere. You might ask why two controls? The first control operates the police alarm. Every Raysons' safe is wired direct to the local police headquarters. The second control opens the safe. So to open the safe, you touch the first pinhead control and that cuts off the police alarm. Then you touch the second pinhead and the safe door slides open. You take your jewels or your bonds or your cash out, pass your finger over the two controls again and the safe shuts and the police alarm is set. Nothing to it ... it's a sweetie."

Both Martha and Henry were sitting forward, listening, absorbed.

Johnny drew on his cigarette, then went on, "If you don't know where the controls are hidden and you try to break open the safe, there is a ray inside the safe that reacts to any violence. It sets off an alarm in the local Cop House and before you can even dent the safe you have three or possibly four cops breathing down your neck. Let's get this straight: the Raysons' safe is probably the best and safest of its kind in the world."

Martha sank back in her chair. She now regretted her heavy breakfast.

"Well, that's wonderful!" she said bitterly. "So all this goddamn work and calculations I've been making is so much waste of time!"

Johnny shook his head.

"No. It can be done. I'd rather open a Raysons' safe than any other safe. What you have to remember is once you know where the two controls are hidden, the safe opens itself. You can open it, take the loot and be away within three minutes. The trick, of course, is to know where the controls are hidden."

Martha perked up.

"Well, go on ... "

"Because the people who buy the safes are rich and lazy and possibly stupid, each local branch have blueprints in their files of each safe they have fitted and where the controls are located. This became a must when some rich old woman forgot where the controls were and the fitter also couldn't remember. What an uproar exploded! I remember it well. She wanted her jewels ... she was entertaining some top brass and she couldn't get at her finery. She sued Raysons and got away with it. So ... " Johnny grinned. "From then on, Raysons have blueprints of every safe fitted. Each local branch keeps their own blueprints. Our next move is to get at the blueprints as we got at this list from Frisby. So let's work it out ... "

That afternoon, Martha and Henry made a call on Paradise City's branch of Raysons' Safes Corporation. Martha explained that she was thinking of building a house in the district and she would want a safe. While David Hacket, the branch manager, was explaining their system, Henry, in his role of a cynic (a lot of damned nonsense ... put your stuff in a safe deposit bank), prowled around the office, checking the locks, the filing cabinets and looking for any wiring that might indicate police alarms. He also checked that there was a photo-copying machine and its make.

Finally, when Martha was sure Henry had all the information he needed, she said she would think it over and call again.

Back at the villa, Henry was gloomy.

"It's tough," he told Johnny. "There are burglar alarms. The four cabinets have metal covers on the locks. I couldn't get an impression. This is a tough one."

Johnny laughed.

"Is that all you found out? I'll tell you what else there is. There's an electric ray that alerts the Cop House if you pass through the ray after office hours. Every door you open alerts the Cop House. If you try to open the safe or any of the filing cabinets another alarm goes off. Raysons are full of gimmicks. I know ... I worked with them, but it doesn't mean a thing. I'll tell you why. Raysons don't rely on the City's supply of electricity. They have their own plant. All you have to do is to cut their motor and their teeth are drawn. Raysons are so pleased with this system they have installed it in every one of their branches. If you don't know, you're a dead duck, but as I do know, I can get to those records."

"No kidding, Johnny?" Martha said, her fat face beaming.

"I know Raysons like I know the back of my hand ... few do. I can get at them."

Martha cut herself a large slice of chocolate cake that Flo had baked the previous day.

"I was getting worried," she admitted. "Henry was so depressed."

"You can still remain worried," Johnny said quietly. He took a pack of cigarettes from his shirt pocket and lit up.

Her mouth full, Martha stared at him. His cold eyes met hers, and she felt a twinge of uneasiness. Hurriedly, she swallowed what she was eating, then asked, "What do you mean?"

There was a long pause. Henry regarded Johnny thoughtfully. Gilda, on her Li-Lo in her white bikini, lifted her head.

Johnny said, "Without me, you three would be sunk. If you think I'm talking out of the back of my neck, say so, and I'll leave you to handle this and then where will you get? Exactly nowhere!"

Martha put down her unfinished slice of cake. She was shrewd enough to realise what this was leading to.

"Go on," she said, her voice harsh. "Finish it."

"You said my share was to be $125,000," Johnny said. He let smoke drift down his nostrils. "The whole take you said was $600,000. Now, I'm telling you something. Without me, you would never even smell $600,000, let alone put your hands on it. So . . . " He paused, looked at Martha, then at Henry. "My cut is to be $200,000, and you can please yourselves how the rest is divided. You can take it or leave it."

"Listen to me, you sonofabitch! If you think . . . " Martha began, her face purple with rage when Henry, speaking sharply, stopped her.

"Martha! I'll handle this!"

Martha stopped short and stared at Henry who was regarding her in his calm, quiet way, his tortoise-like eyelids lowered, his cigar burning evenly between his thin fingers.

"If this creep . . . " Martha began, but Henry again stopped her with a wave of his hand.

"Johnny is right, Martha," he said. "Without him, we can't go ahead with this. He's the technician." He turned to Johnny, his smile benign. "Look, Johnny, suppose we make a little deal. Suppose we settle for $150,000 . . . huh? What do you say? After all, this is Martha's idea. She's behind it all. What do you say . . . $150,000?"

Johnny got to his feet.

"You talk it over among yourselves," he said. "I want

41

$200,000 or you can fix this deal yourselves. I'm going to take a swim."

"So am I," Gilda said and swung herself off the Li-Lo. Johnny ignored her. He walked down the terrace steps and on down to the beach with Gilda after him.

"The creep!" Martha said furiously.

"Now, Martha," Henry said quietly, "that won't get you anywhere. All right, those are his terms. It doesn't mean he will get them, does it? We're not signing any contract with him. He can't sue us, can he?"

Martha stared intently at Henry, then the rage died out of her eyes.

"Do you think you can handle him, Henry?"

"I can but try," Henry said. "I've handled a lot of smart boys in my time. The point is we just can't do without him."

"I had the idea the moment I set eyes on him, we would have trouble with him." Martha was so angry she couldn't finish her cake.

Henry watched Johnny and Gilda as they swam together.

"And another thing, Martha, Gilda has fallen in love with him," he said sadly.

"Do you think I care?"

"I like Gilda ... a pretty girl. I wouldn't want her to get hurt." Then seeing Martha wasn't interested, Henry went on, "When he comes back, I'll say yes to his terms ... right?"

"So long as he doesn't get the money, you can say yes to anything."

"You let me talk to him."

Martha heaved herself to her feet.

"I'm going to take a nap." She hesitated, began to say something, decided not to and stumped off the terrace.

Half an hour later, Johnny and Gilda came up the steps. Johnny paused near Henry.

"Well?"

"It's all right, Johnny. We've talked it over," Henry

said. "Of course, she didn't like it, but she knows when she's licked. You get $200,000."

Johnny stared at him. The cold eyes made Henry a little uneasy, but he retained his calm expression.

"Okay," Johnny said. "But listen ... I know all about you. Abe told me ... one of the smartest con men in the racket. Don't try to con me. That's a warning." He stared again at Henry and then walked off the terrace to his bedroom.

Henry took out his silk handkerchief and touched his temples.

Gilda laid down on the Li-Lo.

"I suppose she's hoping to gyp him," she said, putting on her sun-goggles. "Don't you do it, Henry. I like you. I couldn't care less if he twisted her fat neck, but I don't want anything bad to happen to you."

Henry regarded her beautiful body.

"Thank you, my dear. I wish I were twenty years younger."

Gilda laughed.

"You men ... "

An hour after dinner, Martha came out on to the terrace where Gilda was catching the last rays of the sun and Henry was working on his Stock Exchange calculations.

Johnny had remained in his room for the past three hours. Gilda had seen cigarette smoke drift out of his open window from time to time and she wondered what he was doing. She wasn't worried about her share when the share-out came. She trusted Henry who had promised her ten per cent of the take: that meant, with any luck, $60,000. That would be enough. With that kind of money and with her looks, she reckoned she would never be in want. She admired Johnny for demanding the bigger sum. Anyone who had the guts to stand up to Martha won her admiration.

"Where is he?" Martha demanded, settling herself in the wickerwork chair, causing it to creak.

"In his bedroom," Henry said, putting down his notebook. "Look, Martha, don't let us have any unpleasantness. This boy can handle the job -- we can't. So we must pay for it." The heavy eyelid closed and opened. This little speech Martha realised was for Gilda's benefit.

"Oh, well, all right," she said. "I'll leave it to you," and she picked up her embroidery frame. "We are having Maryland chicken for dinner."

"Good." Henry opened his notebook again. "Flo is one of the best cooks we've ever had. She ... " He paused as Johnny came out on to the terrace.

Johnny was wearing a lightweight blue suit and he was carrying a small overnight bag in his hand. He came across the terrace and stood in front of Martha.

"I want three hundred dollars," he said.

Martha stared at him. Henry put down his notebook, and Gilda half sat up, supporting herself on her arm.

"You want – what?" Martha's voice went up a note.

"Three hundred dollars," he said quietly. "I'm going to Miami. I've got things to fix."

"You're not getting three hundred goddamn dollars out of me!" Martha shrilled, her face turning red.

Johnny stared at her, his eyes ice cold.

"Listen to me, you stupid sow," he said, his voice soft but vicious. "Do you or don't you want to swing this job?"

Martha reared back in her chair as if he had threatened to hit her. Henry got to his feet and walked over to Johnny. He put himself between Johnny and Martha and looked levelly at him.

"That wasn't a nice thing to say, Johnny. You don't talk like that. I won't allow it!"

Johnny half-lifted his clenched fist. Henry remained motionless, looking straight into Johnny's hot, angry eyes. The two men, one frail and old, the other powerful and young, regarded each other for a long moment, then Johnny suddenly grinned and relaxed.

"I like guys with guts," he said. "And that's what you've got, Colonel." He stepped around Henry and said to Martha, "I apologise, but I still need three hundred dollars. I can't walk into Raysons and put their electrics on the blink without money."

Henry took his roll from his hip pocket and gave Johnny three one hundred dollar bills.

"Here you are, son," he said. "What are you planning to do?"

"I'm going to Miami ... I'll be away three days ... Thursday evening we will make the raid."

"That still doesn't tell me what you are planning to do."

"I'll tell you when I come back," Johnny returned, then without looking at either Martha or Gilda, he walked off the terrace.

No one said anything until they heard the Hertz rental car start up and drive away, then Martha said, "I'll fix that sonofabitch if it's the last thing I do."

"Make sure he doesn't fix you first," Gilda said. "I'd back him any day against you!"

"Ladies!" Henry said sharply. "Please ... " He looked at his watch. "It's nearly time for dinner."

The next two days dragged interminably for Gilda. She found life in the villa and in the City flat and dull without Johnny around. She swam and sunbathed and listened to Henry's old-world chat with a boredom that she found intolerable. Martha ate and worked on her embroidery, sullen and bad tempered.

On the evening of the third day, after dinner, they heard a car drive up and they all stiffened, looking at each other. A few minutes later, Johnny came out on to the terrace.

"Welcome back," Henry said. "How did it go?"

Johnny sat down, lit a cigarette and looked directly at Martha. He had given only a casual glance at Gilda who had put on a white linen dress especially for his arrival. Henry, when she came out on to the terrace, declared she looked beautiful, but the impact of her beauty seemed lost on Johnny.

"It's fixed," Johnny said. "I had to put Raysons' electrical equipment on the blink and I had to do it so they wouldn't know. The answer was a time switch clock. I talked it over with Abe. He has contacts everywhere. He sent me to a guy who fitted me out with the uniform of the Paradise City Electricity Corporation. I bought a toolbox on a sling and a time switch clock. Abe sent me to a make-up artist who put fifteen years on my face, plus a moustache. I then went along to Raysons. Their equipment is in the basement and during the day it is not in use. I told the janitor there was a failure and he let me have the run of the basement. It was dead easy. So now, tonight, at nine o'clock, the time switch turns off the electricity. All we have to do is to walk in, find the files, photo-copy them, remove the time switch clock and we're away."

Two days after Johnny had got the blueprints, Martha came down on to the big terrace where the others were reading the papers.

Martha was feeling in good shape. Flo had given her one of her favourite breakfasts, consisting of grapefruit, three lamb chops each set on crisply fried bread, surrounded by a bed of watercress. She couldn't remember when she had had better lamb chops and she was in such a good mood that she even nodded to Johnny instead of scowling at him.

She sat down.

"Now listen to me," she said. "I have a short list here." She waved a sheet of paper. "The trick with this operation is this: we empty the safe and the owners don't know for some weeks that they have been robbed. In this way we can work four or even five safes and we'll be on our way before the cops get into the picture." She paused while the other three regarded her. "There's no miracle in this. Now I've got the names of the people who own good jewellery, I've found out what they are doing and where they are.

There's nothing smart about this: I got the dope from the Society Column of the local rag. For instance, Mrs Lowenstein who owns $180,000 worth of jewellery is in a clinic and she will be there for three weeks. We have the blueprint of her Raysons' safe. We go there, pick up the stuff and Mrs L. won't know she's lost her loot until she's returned from the clinic. So she's the first one we'll hit. Now the second one ... Mrs Warren Crail. She owns $650,000 worth of jewels. At the end of this week, she and her husband are going on a fishing trip and they won't be back for five weeks. So we fix her safe. Then there's Mrs Alex Jackson, who owns $400,000 worth of jewellery. She is also going off on a yacht. There's a chance she will take some of her jewellery with her, but not all of it. All these slobs have faith in the Raysons' safes. So they leave their jewellery ... anyway, why should they worry? It's all insured. Are you getting the photo? There's Mrs Bernard Lampson who owns $350,000 worth of jewels. She is off to the Bahamas for skin diving. She won't be taking her stuff with her, so we'll get it. How do you like it?"

Henry had heard all this before. He nodded and looked across at Johnny who was staring off into space.

"Yes," Johnny said, "if your facts are right."

"This is where Gilda does some work," Martha said. She looked at Gilda. "Now this is what you have to do ... "

Baines had been Mrs Lowenstein's butler for ten years. He was an import from England and in the past had served two of the best titled families during his sixty-eight years. He had been seduced by the enormous salary Mrs Lowenstein had offered him and he had agreed to come to Paradise City to run her establishment ... he had regretted it ever since.

However, he was a man of integrity and he also had a conscience so in return for his salary that was five times as much as any English Duke could afford to pay him, he endured Mrs Lowenstein's vulgarity, her shrieking voice, her dreadful clothes and her frightful friends.

Happily, every year, Mrs Lowenstein went into a health clinic where they worked on her bulk and generally cleaned her inside and out, and then returned her after a month to her magnificent home to begin eating and drinking again with renewed vigour. Baines looked forward to this month when he had the house to himself. The rest of the staff took their vacation at this time. Everything was put under dust wraps and Baines settled down happily in his suite on the top floor that consisted of a bedroom, a sitting-room, a bathroom and a kitchenette. Baines was a TV addict. He spent nearly all his free time staring at the lighted screen.

Around eleven-thirty one morning as he was arranging his lunch with loving hands, he heard the front doorbell ring.

Baines was in his shirt sleeves, but he was always immaculately dressed. He was a short, stout, pink-faced man with snowy, thin hair and calm blue eyes – the perfect picture of what an English butler should look like. He frowned, turned off the gas that was heating the *Coq au Vin* he had prepared the previous day, put on his tail-coat and went down in the elevator to the front door.

A dark haired, severely dressed girl stood on the doorstep. She wore a blue frock with white collar and cuffs and heavy sun-goggles. Her jet black hair made a neat helmet for her well-shaped head.

The wig and the dress completely transformed Gilda into an efficient, serious-looking young business woman.

"I am from the Acme Carpet Cleaning Co.," she said and handed Baines a printed card that Abe had supplied.

Baines read the card with an aristocratic lift of his eyebrows. "I think there must be a mistake ... " he began.

"Mrs Lowenstein telephoned from the clinic," Gilda explained. "Mrs Lowenstein has asked for an estimate for us to clean the carpet in the main living-room and also the carpet in her bedroom."

As Mrs Lowenstein never ceased to use the telephone at the clinic this came as no surprise to Baines. Many a time when he was enjoying a good TV serial the telephone would ring and he would have to listen to Mrs Lowenstein's whining complaints with one eye on the TV screen.

"I understand," he said and opened the front door wide. "What do you want to do?"

"May I see both carpets? I will have to measure them for the estimate."

Baines liked the look of this girl. She was neat and respectful. He approved of her. He let her in and watched her as she measured the living-room carpet with a foot rule. Then he took her up to Mrs Lowenstein's bedroom where all the furniture in the enormous room was under dust sheets.

Gilda measured the carpet and as she closed her notebook, she said, "Mrs Lowenstein won't be back then for a few days?"

"Madame won't be back for at least three weeks," Baines said, thinking Glory be! but not saying it.

"That gives us plenty of time." Gilda smiled brightly. "We will send Mrs Lowenstein the estimate and if she agrees it, I'll let you know when we can collect the carpets. Would that be all right?"

Pleased with her good manners, Baines said that would be quite all right. As he conducted her down in the elevator, she said, "Are you all alone here?"

"Yes," Baines said with a contented sigh. "The rest of the staff are on vacation."

"I'm sure you appreciate the quiet," Gilda said, moving from the elevator. "It must be nice to be on one's own for a little while – especially in such a beautiful house."

Baines warmed to her.

"It's a pleasure." He opened the front door. "I always say you can never be lonely with the telly."

"Are you a fan?" Gilda turned and looked through her sun-goggles at him. "So am I. When I get home, I turn it on and that's it until I go to bed. Good-bye."

Baines watched her walk down the steps to the white Opel car. Then remembering he had his *Coq au Vin* to heat up, he shut the front door, shot the bolt and took the elevator up to his quarters.

That night Johnny and Gilda raided the house. Gilda had no trouble in climbing to the first floor. Johnny stood in the moon-light and watched her as she went up the side of the house as if she were walking up a flight of stairs. She lowered a knotted rope down to him and he came up that way, hand over hand, joining her on the balcony. She had described to him the lock on the window and Johnny had brought along the necessary tools to open it.

With the blueprint from Raysons, it took them only a few minutes to locate the controls, another minute or so to open the safe. Both wore surgical gloves. Johnny emptied the glittering gems from their cases into the small sack he had brought with him. The job lasted less than five minutes. Then they left. Johnny relocked the window from the outside, then they slid down the rope, jerked it free and were away.

The first raid of the big take was accomplished.

CHAPTER THREE

"To get this story in its right perspective," Al Barney said, "I now have to take you back three years. We'll come up to date before long, but I want you to get it into your mind, we are going back three years."

I said I understood.

Al nodded and took some beer.

"Well, now ... I want to tell you about Harry Lewis ...

"At the age of thirty-eight, Harry Lewis became the husband of one of the richest women in the world. He didn't make any effort to marry her – she married him. The moment she set eyes on him, he was a dead duck. She wanted him as her husband, and when Lisa Cohen wanted anything, she always got it. Harry wasn't anything special in the brainbox line nor was he particularly bright in business. But he had looks. He was one of those tall, husky, handsome guys you see on the movies – a Gregory Peck type. He had loads of personality, sex appeal and a smile that rocked the kind of girls he associated with. Make no mistake about it, Harry had a stable full of girls who dropped flat on their backs when he gave the signal. But apart from his looks, Harry was no great shakes, and he was grateful that more by luck than hard work, he had become the manager of one of Cohen's Self-Service Stores, right here in Paradise City." Al paused to look at me. "Maybe you've heard of Sol Cohen?"

I said I had heard of him – who hadn't?

"Yeah ... well, here was Harry walking around the store, showing his teeth to the girls who worked there, giving some of them who would stand for it a quick feel when no one was looking and earning around six thousand dollars a year. He had more or less made up his mind he wouldn't get beyond this income bracket, and this was as far as he would go in his career. This didn't worry him too much ... he wasn't the ambitious type. With six grand coming in steadily, he could amuse himself, have all the girls he wanted and pay the rent of a two-room apartment that faced the sea and that was pretty cosy over the week-ends when he would sun himself on the balcony with a girl on his lap or near enough for him to reach for should the idea come into his mind.

"I don't ever want you to imagine Harry was dumb. No one who ever worked for Sol Cohen could be dumb, but Harry wasn't anything special. He did his job and got by.

"Well, one hot, sunny afternoon something happened that was to turn his life upside down and inside out. Imagine Harry wandering around the store, keeping his eyes on things, giving his favourites his sexy look, pausing to have a word with the customers, feeling like a captain on his ship when the sea is nice and calm, when a woman comes up to him.

"I've seen Lisa Cohen a number of times, so let me describe her to you. She was small, dark and skinny. She had big eyes – her best feature – and her father's nose that took up most of her face. She had a mouth and chin that showed temper and aggression. One thing you can be certain about, Lisa Cohen would never make the centre spread in *Playboy*. You could bet your last buck on that and not have a sleepless night. At the time she first met Harry she was twenty-nine years of age. She was wearing a pair of white slacks and a blue sweat shirt that made her look like a half-grown teenager.

"She was in Paradise City on a month's vacation. The Cohens' home was in 'Frisco, and this was her first visit to Paradise City. She had been there two weeks with friends on her father's yacht and the old man had asked her to take a gander at the store to see how it was being handled and to report back to him. He had a lot of faith in Lisa's judgement and he got her to do these snap checks when she was in Florida. A couple of times, she had reported unfavourably, and the managers of the stores found themselves out on the cold, hard sidewalk.

"Lisa had been watching Harry without him noticing her for the past ten minutes. She had been wandering around the store, noting how the merchandise was being displayed, how the girls coped, and she had been favourably impressed. She was still more impressed when she realised this tall, husky hunk of beautiful manhood was the store manager.

"It's no secret that Lisa had hot pants. I wouldn't go so far as to say she was a nympho, but she was as near it as makes no difference. She could have married twenty or thirty times. With her money, and what Sol Cohen was going to leave her, men were queueing up. Lisa let a lot of them lay her. This was something she had to have, but she had made up her mind when she was going to marry she would pick her man for herself and he wasn't marrying her just for her loot.

"As soon as she saw Harry, she decided he was the one she was going to marry. Up to now, she had met all types of men: tall, thin, short, fat, smooth, brash, young and old, but none of them combined Harry's looks, his huskiness and the sex appeal that leaked out of his ears.

"So she went up to him, looking at him with her big, alive eyes and told him who she was."

To say Harry was startled to find himself face to face with his boss's daughter was to put it mildly. He was practically thrown into a panic. He wondered how long she had been in the store . . . if she had seen him squeeze the bottom of the girl working on the cosmetic counter. He wondered . . . then he pulled himself together and switched on his charming smile.

"Welcome to the store, Miss Cohen. This is an unexpected pleasure."

Lisa had noted the panic, which pleased her. She also liked the smile which made her blood move more quickly.

"I want to talk to you about the store," she said abruptly. "What time do you close?"

"Seven o'clock," Harry told her. "Won't you come up to the office, Miss Cohen?"

"I'll be outside in my car at seven," Lisa said. "We will have dinner together," and turning, she walked into the crowd and Harry lost sight of her.

He cursed to himself because he had a girl lined up who promised great things for this night, but he had no alternative but to call her and cancel the date. She took it badly. Harry said it was just one of those things and hung up while she was still screaming abuse.

During the afternoon, he wondered what the hell the daughter of a tycoon wanted, having dinner with him. He spent the rest of the afternoon in his office, feverishly making notes on the latest sales figures and getting out a balance sheet. He could only imagine she was going to probe his profit and loss account, and as the takings had fallen off during the month, Harry sweated. But he need not have worried. During dinner, Lisa didn't even mention the store.

She was waiting for him in a white Aston Martin. she had changed into a simple scarlet dress which from its cut must have cost plenty. She wore no jewellery and no stockings. Her black glossy hair was immaculate and if her nose had allowed her to look attractive, she would have been attractive.

Harry got into the passenger's seat and she shot the car off with an expertise change of gears that startled him. She said nothing until they were roaring along the beach road that led out of Paradise City, then she asked abruptly, "Can you eat sea food?"

"Why, sure," Harry said. "I can eat anything."

She concentrated on her driving, and although Harry hated to be driven, preferring always to drive himself, he didn't feel one qualm of uneasiness although she drove at an enormous speed.

They arrived at a small restaurant that Harry knew to be murderously expensive, situated on a lonely strip of beach. He wondered if he had enough money on him to meet the check, but again he need not have worried. When the *Maitre d'hotel* saw Lisa, he came forward, bowing, and led them to a secluded booth, away from the rest of the crowded restaurant and from then on, Harry had nothing to do with the arrangements.

The dinner had already been ordered: king-sized prawns, hanging from wine glasses that were filled with crushed ice, lobster in a cream and champagne sauce, followed by wild strawberries in Kirsch.

During the meal, Lisa, sitting opposite Harry, studied him and questioned him: not about the store as he had expected, but about himself. Her questions were personal and probing, and bewildered, Harry answered them. Who were his parents? What was his father's profession? Where was he educated? What were his ambitions? (To this, Harry answered a little vaguely that he was doing all right at the store and liked the work. Then seeing Lisa's sharp, frowning stare, he went on to say that of course it would be grand to get to head office, but he did really enjoy his work.) Was he married? What were his hobbies? (To this, Harry said golf, but if he had told the truth, he would have said sex.) The probing questions went on and on and Harry became more bewildered and even a little resentful, but he told himself you never know: she might be vetting him for a more important job.

By the end of the dinner, Lisa knew almost as much about Harry as he did himself – but not quite. When she abruptly asked him about his sex life, Harry threw up a smoke screen. This was taking the probe just too far.

"I get along ... is this something we have to talk about?"

She studied him, then nodded.

"No. Do you want coffee?"

"Look, Miss Cohen," Harry said firmly, feeling now was the time to assert himself. "You are my guest. I want you to understand that. Do *you* want coffee?"

She moved her shoulders impatiently.

"Don't be a fool," she said with brutal curtness. "It goes down on Daddy's account. I sign for everything and he pays. On what you earn, you couldn't possibly afford to pay the check ... do you want coffee?"

Thinking back later, Harry realised this was the crucial moment when he should have either slapped her face or tossed his only $100 bill on the table and walked out. But Harry wasn't made of that stuff. He hesitated, then turned on his charm.

"Why, thanks ... I didn't know. A coffee would be marvellous."

From that moment, he was a dead duck.

They had coffee and brandy and they discussed the latest novels, the latest pop discs and the latest movies. All the time, he felt those big black eyes searching his face, regarding the width of his shoulders, looking intently at his hands.

Then suddenly she signalled to the *Maitre d'hotel* for the check. She examined it carefully, even added the figures, then she signed it. She put a ten dollar bill on the plate as a tip. As she left the restaurant, money passed between her and the *Maitre d'hotel*. He bowed nearly to the floor. Harry registered this and flinched. This was brash, vulgar spending and he resented it.

They walked together to the car. Harry said it was one of the best meals he had had, and he thanked her for it. Lisa said nothing. She got in the car, started the engine and when Harry was by her side, she drove the car further down the beach road towards the sand dunes.

"I don't know if you know it," Harry said awkwardly, "but this road is a dead-end. You ... "

"I know," she said.

Because Harry wasn't all that dumb, he got the idea that the evening wasn't over. He suddenly realised Lisa Cohen, his boss's daughter, had hot pants for him, and this brought him out in a cold sweat. For one thing, she wasn't his type. She was just the kind of girl Harry never even looked at. He liked his girls to have big breasts and neat, hard bottoms. This girl had no front and no behind. She was just skinny. Apart from that, he thought of Sol Cohen. If he laid his daughter and Cohen heard about it, he would be out on his ear.

Lisa pulled up under a clump of palm trees. There was a big stretch of silver sand, looking in the moonlight like freshly laundered sheet ... there was the sea.

She got out of the car and walked down on to the hard firm sand, and Harry, his heart thumping, feeling he wanted to shout for help, followed her. She sat down under the palm trees and he stood over her.

She looked up at him.

"Come on," she said impatiently, "take me."

A half an hour later, Harry came out of an exhausted doze and stared up at the big, white moon. He felt as if he had been put through a wringer. Never before in his sexual life had he ever had such an experience. Making love with Lisa was like making love to a buzz-saw. It had been a shattering session and Harry had hated it. When he laid a girl, he liked to be in charge. He liked to regulate the tempo, but he had had no chance to do anything but to submit to Lisa's terrifying passion.

"Give me a cigarette," she said. She had pulled down her dress and was lying placidly by his side. As he lit the cigarette for her, he was surprised to see in the flame of the lighter how relaxed she was now. The hardness had gone. As she looked at him, smiling, her eyes limpid and kind, in spite of the size of her nose, she looked beautiful.

Not knowing what to say, still feeling torn to pieces, Harry said nothing. He lay there until Lisa had finished her cigarette, then she crushed it out into the sand and sat up.

"I must get back. They'll think I've had an accident or something," She got to her feet and walked across the sand to the car. Harry followed her. It was an effort to drag one foot after the other. He had never felt so drained out.

As she slid under the steering wheel and as he dropped heavily into the passenger's seat, she looked inquiringly at him.

"Was it good?" she asked.

Harry could have said it was sheer hell, but he remembered his job. After all, he told himself, she would soon be gone. This was something not to be repeated, so he lied: "The best ever."

She nodded, slid into gear and sent the car roaring back along the beach road towards the lights of the City.

Three days later when Harry had recovered his virility and had had no word from Lisa, he decided he was out of danger. This was just a passing thing, he assured himself, and he wouldn't have to face that ordeal again.

When Lisa had said good-bye to him, she had looked intently at him with those big, glittering eyes and had smiled. "It *was* good, wasn't it, Harry? It was the best ever for me too." Then she had driven away.

Well, that was that, Harry thought with heart-felt relief. What an experience ... phew!

But how wrong he was.

On this third day, he was in his office working on re-order sheets when the telephone rang.

"This is Miss Selby," a cool, crisp voice informed him. "Mr Cohen's personal secretary. I am calling from San Francisco. Mr Cohen wants to see you at three o'clock on Friday, the 11th. I have mailed you your return air ticket. It will reach you tomorrow. Please be punctual," and the line went dead.

Right then and there, Harry laid an egg. The few times

any store manager had been summoned to the holy of holies, he had got the gate. Could the old bastard have heard about Lisa? Harry wondered, really sweating it out. If he got the gate, what was he going to do? He hadn't saved any money ... damn it, he owed money! Hell's teeth! He would be fixed!

By the time he reached 'Frisco and had been shot up seventeen floors in the express elevator to Sol Cohen's palatial office, he was practically a hospital case.

He was met by Miss Selby who he had heard about. She was tall and willowy and gorgeous, with eyes like ice pick points and a smile that would have frozen a glacier. She took him to Sol Cohen's office door, tapped and half-opened the door.

Harry heard a voice talking with vicious anger. The sound of the voice sent a chill up his spine.

Sol Cohen was on the telephone.

"German?" Sol Cohen was shouting. "Listen, Sam, don't tell me lies like that! That consignment comes from China! I know! You can't fool me! I'm not handling any crap from China!" There was a click as Cohen slammed down the receiver.

Miss Selby raised her beautiful eyebrows at Harry, her face expressionless.

"You may go in."

Sol Cohen was a small, fat, balding man with a big hooked nose, small, dark, tough-looking eyes and the magic only the real top executives have that come from them like a laser ray.

As Harry walked across the forty-foot carpet before he finally arrived at Cohen's desk which was big enough to play billiards on, Cohen leaned back on his high executive chair and studied him. By the time Harry reached the desk, his knees were knocking together and he was sweating cold sweat.

Cohen's fat face was a hard mask: an unnerving face. Harry thought wildly that this could be a dead face, then the face broke into a wide beaming smile and Cohen became transformed from a ruthless tycoon to a jovial, fat Jew who wouldn't hurt a fly.

"You Harry Lewis?" he said, getting to his feet.

Harry gaped at him. The transformation threw him hopelessly out of his stride.

"Y-yes, sir."

"Sit down, boy. First, let me shake your hand."

Dazed, Harry felt the small hard hand grip his, then as Cohen waved to a chair opposite his desk, he almost collapsed into it.

"So you're Harry Lewis." Cohen regarded him, smiling, then he nodded. "Quite a boy! Well! Well! I always knew Lisa could pick 'em. Now listen, Harry, I've got a busy day. People keep worrying me. When you run a business the way I run this business, you're like a goddam slave, so we'll have to make this a quickie. Maybe when I take a vacation, we'll get together and have fun ... huh?"

Harry just stared at him.

"You want a cigar?" Cohen asked.

"No-no, thank you, sir."

"Okay, Harry, let's get at it. Tell me, how do you like the idea of me being your father-in-law?"

Harry thought: One of us must be mad! I guess it must be me!

'Surprised? Didn't Lisa tell you?" Cohen laughed. "My little girl loves you ... you love her ... so ... okay. She wants to marry you and when Lisa wants anything, she gets it." Cohen wagged his head, his expression rueful. "I'll tell you something, Harry, she's got me wrapped around her finger. But I like the idea of Lisa getting married. I want grandchildren. You know something, Harry? I like little kids. It's the Jew in me. Besides, I'm not going to last for ever and I want to leave my dough to Lisa and after her to three or four or even five boys. See."

Harry was speechless. He just sat there, sweat beading his face, his heart thumping, his mouth half-open.

"I've been checking on your record, Harry," Cohen went on. "No great shakes, huh? Six thousand ... nothing, but according to Lisa you've got something pretty special." He gave a leering laugh, "And Lisa likes it. Between you and me ... how was she?"

Harry reared back, feeling blood rush to his face.

"I'd rather ... I ... I ... "

Cohen waved his hand.

"Okay, boy ... I like that ... shows class," he said. "Forget it ... sure, that's something a classy guy doesn't talk about. Well now, Harry, I've got to rush this. I've a full day. Just listen: Lisa wants to get married at the end of the month. I've already got a replacement for you at the store. That'll give you a chance to help Lisa find a house. She's struck with Paradise City and wants to settle there. I'll miss her here, but when Lisa wants anything, she damn well gets it. So she'll look around and she'll find a house. You must be around to help her. The house and everything that goes with it ... the furniture ... the cars ... you know, is all on me. I'm opening a bank account down there with the Florida Deposit in your joint names ... just to start you two off right. I thought two hundred and fifty thousand. When the account begins to run low – and knowing Lisa – it'll run low – I'll keep it topped up. You have nothing to worry about. When you get back, go along to the bank and draw some money. Buy some clothes. When you go around with Lisa you've got to look good." The telephone bell buzzed and Cohen scowled. When he scowled, Harry shivered. It was a different face: a face you see in a nightmare. Cohen snatched up another telephone receiver. "I'm busy! I'm not taking calls! What? Hong Kong? Who the hell cares about Hong Kong?" and he slammed down the receiver. For a long moment he scowled at the telephone, then he worked himself into a good mood again. "What was I saying? Oh, yeah. Now look, Harry, I don't believe a man can be happy without some kind of work. Lisa didn't want you to work. She thought you should stick around in the house and on the yacht and have fun with her, but I don't go for that. I think you should have some work to do. I've got fifty thousand acres of building land out in Florida. My father bought it for a song. I've sat on it for years, but three months ago, I began to sell. I've set up an office in Paradise City. The punk in charge is as useless as a new-born babe – all he does is to make a noise. So I telephoned him this morning and gave him the heave-ho." Harry suppressed a shiver. "When a guy is no use to me, I get rid of him," Cohen went on, "and this punk has a hole in his head. Well now, Harry, here's a job that'll give you interest. It's not hard. There's a clever little bitch down there who knows all the answers. She practically runs the office on her own, but I like a man in the front. I thought twenty thousand would be about right ... we can adjust that later. That'll be your own personal spending money. Of course, the heavy money will come from your joint account. The other money is for your cigarettes. Get all this?"

Still Harry said nothing, but by now his mind was beginning to function.

Two hundred and fifty thousand dollars ... a house ... a yacht ... $20,000 a year ... a job in an office.

Miss Selby put her gorgeous head around the door.

"Excuse me, Mr Cohen, but the American Ambassador is calling from London and Hong Kong is still on the line."

Cohen raised his hands and grimaced at Harry.

"You see, boy ... no peace. Well, okay, you get back to Paradise City and clear up. Lisa will be down in a couple of days. Excuse me, huh? I know you two are going to be very, very happy."

Harry felt a touch on his arm from Miss Selby and he got slowly to his feet. He left the office as Cohen began talking on one of his many telephones.

Miss Selby eyed Harry over. Her eyes were hostile, her smile freezing.

"Congratulations, Mr Lewis," she said and went to her desk.

Harry walked to the elevator. He moved like a man under a shock.

During the three weeks that Harry remained a bachelor, every now and then, he decided to cut and run, but he hadn't the guts. The prize was too glittering. When he saw the house Lisa had chosen, his eyes nearly fell out of his head. It had eight bedrooms, eight bathrooms, four living-rooms, a magnificent garden and swimming pool . . . the whole works. There was a Rolls, a Caddy and the Aston Martin in the garage. There was a Jap butler, a housekeeper and five other staff and three Chinese gardeners. There was a yacht which had luxury accommodation for twenty people . . . a small liner. Suddenly Harry was handed on a plate everything a man could dream of, but he also had Lisa.

While he was clearing out his desk in the small poky office at the self-service store, the day following his interview with Sol Cohen, the door opened and Lisa came in. She shut the door and turned the key. She came across to where Harry was standing and looked up at him, her dark eyes shining. "Hello, Harry," Lisa said and smiled. "Surprised?"

By now, Harry had made his decision. Whatever else he might have been, he was honest and he was now determined, since Lisa had bought him, he would somehow give her value for her money. He knew what she wanted, and if it half-killed him, he would give it to her. All the way back from 'Frisco, he had thought about the deal. At first, he had decided to pack his bag and get the hell out. Then he thought what it could mean to be the husband of the heir to the Cohen millions. The scale was too heavily balanced in Lisa's favour, but often when he lay in bed in the dark and thought of what he was heading for, he still wanted to run, but he didn't.

So now with this small, unattractive, enormously wealthy woman standing in front of him, Harry did what was expected of him.

"Surprised?" He laughed. "I'm crazy with joy!" He pulled her to him, slid his hands up under her dress and captured her small, skinny buttocks in either hand. "I'm going to make you happy, Lisa," he said, and held her hard against him.

"Sol Cohen came down for the wedding. There were close on eight hundred guests . . . it was one of the biggest turnouts in Paradise City. Sol was in tremendous form. He brought with him his personal present for the bride . . . the Esmaldi necklace."

Here Al Barney paused and regarded me with a cocked eyebrow.

"I told you I'd finally get around to the necklace, didn't I? Well, let me tell you about it. The Esmaldi necklace belonged to one of those South American dictators who are always in trouble. He had to get out fast . . . so fast, all he took with him was his wife's necklace that had been in the family for a couple of generations. He ran into Sol Cohen and Sol bought the necklace off him. No one knows what he paid for it. Sol stashed it away, planning to give it to Lisa as a wedding present. The necklace consisted of one hundred matched diamonds the size of garden peas. The setting was platinum and the lot – so the newspapers said – was worth around three hundred and fifty thousand dollars.

"Lisa wore it at the wedding. Then she put it in her Raysons' safe and went off on the honeymoon in the yacht to the Bahamas.

"She and Harry cruised for a month. During that time Harry gave her value for money. Lisa practically killed him. She was insatiable. There were times when he wanted to jump overboard and swim ashore, but he didn't.

"When the mood hit her, and sometimes it would hit her two or three times a day, she would look directly at him and say, 'Harry . . . ' Then she would leave her lounging chair and walk down to their cabin. Harry would follow like a sheep to the slaughter.

"He had what she wanted and he gave it to her. If only she had been attractive! Harry often thought, but she was bony, her breasts were like poached eggs and her ribs showed, but at least she had technique! Boy! Had she technique!

"After two weeks, Harry was longing to get off the yacht. If the goddamn yacht had struck a reef, he would have cheered with joy. But finally, like everything in this world, things had to come tó an end, and they moved into their new, palatial home.

"It was better then because Harry began to work at the downtown office. He had only Lisa in his hair from six o'clock in the evening onwards, but that was bad enough. He discovered there were two things that Lisa was mad about: he getting astride her and she getting astride a horse. She practically lived on a horse when he was in the office. She had three thoroughbreds and she was always out in the woods or galloping along the bridle paths, either on her own or with other women who were also horse crazy.

"In the evenings, there were always parties: either thrown by Lisa or thrown by someone else. Harry was a great party man and he was popular. On the face of it, the marriage seemed to be going well. It was bed time that Harry feared. But so long as he did his duty, he found Lisa surprisingly easy to live with. It was doing his duty that stuck in his throat.

"He hoped Lisa would get enough of sex to cool off as the time went on, but she didn't. She just couldn't get enough of him. There were times when it drove Harry crazy. There were times too when he unexpectedly ran into some of his past girlfriends who gave him the eye and he knew he had only to return the signal to have someone who really had a body and not a piece of scrawn, but Harry was honest. He knew the value of what he was getting and he was determined not to cheat – besides, he was so handled by Lisa, the urge just wasn't there.

"Every so often, when the party was grand enough, Lisa would wear the Esmaldi diamonds. The necklace made the other women tear their hair with envy. Watching her, Harry thought sadly what a waste of beauty it was. She just didn't have the face or the neck to carry the necklace off. He got so he hated the necklace. There were times when one of the real beauties of Paradise City – and there were a number of them – was at a party and Harry longed to take the necklace off Lisa's scraggy neck and put it on this particular beauty. He was sure the effect would have been out of this world.

"He wasn't too happy working in the office, handling Cohen's fifty thousand acres of land. The office itself was pretty nice: very luxe and his own private office top executive. But selling or trying to sell parcels of land bored Harry. He didn't understand high pressure selling. He found it difficult to enthuse over maps and he wasn't very good with customers who were suspicious.

"He also disliked Harriet Bernstein, his secretary. Cohen had said she practically ran the business, and she did. She was around thirty-eight, short, fat, neatly dressed with a small hooked nose, beady, black eyes and a complexion like mutton fat. Harry knew, as soon as they first met, she neither liked him nor trusted him. His charm bounced off her like a golf ball slammed against a concrete wall. She was terrifyingly efficient. He had only to ask for a letter, a plan, a title deed to have it on his desk before the words were scarcely out of his mouth. She knew the credit rating of every customer. She knew who was worth a business lunch and who wasn't. She had arranged for a table at the Yacht Club to be permanently at Harry's disposal, and every morning when he came into his office, he found a neatly typed memo showing him his appointments and who he was lunching with and all the necessary details about his guest. He could understand Sol Cohen appreciating this kind of service, but it stifled Harry.

There were times when some congenial customer came to see him who he would have liked to have taken to some waterfront sea food restaurant instead of the grand Yacht Club, but he just hadn't the nerve to upset Miss Bernstein's carefully planned schedule.

"So Harry wasn't all that happy at the office and not all that happy at home. At one time, before he married Lisa, he thought she would turn out to be a first-class bitch, but this wasn't so. So long as the bed arrangements worked smoothly, Lisa was even fun.

"They had been married for two years when the accident happened. During this time, Harry had got a better grasp of the business and had sold some thirty acres of building land which pleased Sol as the price was high. Harry was now used to luxury living. Because of him, Lisa's parties were considered the best in the City. She, herself, was never too popular. She bored men, and the women envied her too much, but everyone liked Harry. Every so often they would go off on the yacht with a party. Harry learned to skin dive." Here Al Barney paused. "I taught him. He took to it like a fish. Well, anyway, he found life wasn't all that bad, and after all, he was husky enough to satisfy Lisa, and she really doted on him.

"After some trouble, he had finally sold a parcel of land to an Englishman who was looking for a place in the sun. He had exchanged contracts, shaken hands, and as his customer left the office, Harry sat back in his chair, feeling he wasn't doing too badly. He decided he would take Lisa out that night to celebrate when Miss Bernstein came in. There was something about her fat face that made Harry stiffen. Usually, she was placid and coldly efficient, but now her face looked like mutton fat that had been dropped on the floor.

"Dr Gourley wants to speak to you," she said, and her voice was shrill.

Dr Gourley was their personal doctor. Lisa liked doctors, and was constantly having check-ups and making Harry have them too.

Harry stared at her.

"Dr Gourley?"

"There's been an accident," Miss Bernstein said, and to his horror began to cry.

Harry snatched up the telephone receiver.

It appeared that Lisa had been thrown from her horse. Some dog had run across the bridle path and the horse had shied violently.

The grave, quiet voice of the doctor sent a cold chill up Harry's spine.

"She's at my clinic, Mr Lewis. It's bad. Will you come at once?"

The accident fixed Lisa. She came down on a hunk of rock and jolted her spine out of shape. From that moment Lisa was a cripple from the waist down. Harry's world turned upside down and inside out again. At first, he couldn't believe what the doctor was telling him. Then it dawned on him there would be no more bed sessions, and he felt as if a ton of rock had been taken off his back. Then he felt shocked to think that Lisa wouldn't walk again. Then finally, but this came later, he realised he was chained to a cripple.

When Sol Cohen got the news, he had a fatal heart attack. He was dead before the snooty Miss Selby could reach a telephone to get help.

Harry practically panicked when he heard that Sol Cohen was dead. What with Lisa in the clinic, semi-conscious and now Sol dead, he imagined he would have the Cohen kingdom to deal with. But he quickly found out that Sol had taken care of everything. There was a Vice-President, a board of directors, lawyers, three hatchet-faced Trustees – all of them just waved Harry away and handled everything.

It wasn't until Lisa came out of the clinic in a wheelchair that Sol's will was read. Everything went to Lisa. Harry wasn't even mentioned. Sol might just as well have been alive for all the difference it made to Harry.

But Lisa's accident did make a change in Harry's life.

When the fact finally sank into her mind that she would never get laid again and would never ride a horse again, she went a little crazy in the head.

Harry had always suspected that there was a bitch in her, and now the bitch came out into the open. From the moment she returned to the house, Harry's life turned into a nightmare. The red light went up when she closed their joint account and reopened it in her name only.

"Daddy has left everything to me," she said, staring at Harry, "so I am going to run everything. You have your money for cigarettes. I'm handling the rest of the money."

There were no more parties. *Who the hell wants to come here with me in this goddam wheelchair?* Harry tried to talk her out of this mood without success. *Do you imagine I'm going to entertain all those so-called glamorous whores so you can give them a sly feel? And listen ... while we are on the subject of whores ... if I can't have it, you're not having it! I warn you! Do you understand?* Harry, shaken, said feebly, "Don't talk like that, darling. This is as big a tragedy for me as it is for you." She glared at him, her big eyes glittering. "Okay ... so keep it a tragedy for you, Harry, or you're out!"

Two years of luxury living had not only made a big impact on Harry, it had also softened him. The thought of being out of a job, out of this beautiful house, out of his top executive office scared him silly.

But at the back of his mind, he felt, if he really had to get laid, he would be able to manage it so discreetly that Lisa would never know. But he quickly found out that he was now surrounded by spies. Miss Bernstein, To-To, the Japanese butler and Helgar were always spying on him.

Helgar was Lisa's nurse – a gaunt, tall Dane, around fifty-five with flaxen hair, a face like a horse and eyes like stone. Harry got the idea that this woman disliked him and would, if she could, stir up trouble for him. In his turn, he hated her.

During the day, Lisa kept busy on the telephone in

contact with 'Frisco, her bank and her lawyers and driving Miss Selby crazy. Harry had the satisfaction of knowing that she was just as bitchy to these people as she was to him. But it was the evenings and the week-ends that Harry dreaded. After he had returned from work, he never knew in what mood he would find Lisa. Sometimes she would be reasonable, but always complaining, but most times she was sheer hell.

In despair, one evening after she had snapped off the TV set and had flung her novel across the room, Harry had suggested they should have a party. "It would do you good," he said. "You can't go on living . . . "

"Shut up!" Lisa screamed at him. "Do you think I want those creeps coming here and pitying me! If I'm caught, then you're caught, and if you don't like it, then get the hell out of here!"

That's how their life together was for the next few months. Things happened. For instance, Harry had got into the habit of buying clothes when he wanted them. He bought three light-weight suits, charged them to the joint account, forgetting the joint account no longer existed. The scene that followed him alerted him as to how bad Lisa's mental state had become.

When he returned home after a day in the office, Lisa threw the bills at him. "Pay them yourself!" she screamed at him. "You have your own money! How dare you charge these to my account!"

Harry remembered there wasn't much in his account. Twenty thousand dollars a year sounded all right, but when he had to find his cigarettes, his drinks, his gas for the car, take care of the big tips at the Yacht Club and all the other incidentals of a rich man, there wasn't much left. He realised the tailor's bill would have to wait until he received his next monthly cheque from the Trustees.

But there were also times when Lisa was pathetic. When she got rid of Helgar and was alone in her vast, ornate bedroom. This was the time when she was in the mood when she allowed Harry to comfort her, and because he was strictly honest, he made the effort and did his best. There were times when she asked him to open the Raysons' safe and give her the Esmaldi necklace. She would put it on and wheel herself to the mirror and stare at herself and then weep bitterly. When she cried she shook as if her sobs would tear her to pieces and Harry felt pretty bad about this.

Finally, after two months had dragged by, he risked an explosion and suggested that they went on the yacht and get the hell out of the house for a while. To his surprise, Lisa agreed. She was now getting sick of pitying herself. Harry then suggested they should take along with them a few of their close friends. He was careful to suggest three women who had as much charm as a dentist's drill and their husbands who lived for horses. Again Lisa agreed.

The cruise was a success. A few days after their return, Lisa told Harry that she was going to throw a party. She had decided no one gave a damn that she was chained to a wheelchair so long as they could get drunk and eat the luxury food she provided . . . so, what the hell?

Life then slowly came back to normal for Harry, but he had to be careful. It was like living with a time bomb in his lap. During any party, he dared not move far from Lisa's chair. He had always to be near her or there would be a nerve shattering scene after the party. After some six months living like a monk, Harry found the sex urge getting on top of him, but he fought it off. He knew this was asking for the worst kind of trouble: besides, he couldn't see how he could even hire a whore! He just had no opportunity. He left home at ten a.m. for the office and he knew Miss Bernstein, the spy, would telephone Lisa if he was even half an hour late. His lunch hour was given up to feeding clients. He returned home at six p.m. The rest of the evening was spent with Lisa until she went to bed at ten-thirty. Then he was on his own, but he knew Helgar and To-To were prowling around and there was no chance of sneaking out. Anyway, in spite of this urge, there was no one woman in Paradise City he knew of worth fooling with at the risk of losing this luxury standard of life. So Harry gritted his teeth and remained celibate.

This situation went on for another two months. Then Harry got a break. Lisa had thrown a small party and among the guests was Jack English. He was like Harry: married to a rich woman and scared silly of putting a foot wrong. English was nice: a quiet guy and Lisa liked him. He wasn't much to look at: tall, thin with a face like a spaniel, but nice. He said suddenly to Lisa, "You know something? Harry's getting fat. The trouble with him is he isn't taking any exercise. I'm looking for a golfing partner. Don't you think he should get off some of that fat?" As Lisa hesitated, Harry's heart stood still, then she looked at him: she was in one of her good moods. "Do you want to take up golf again, Harry?" she asked. He forced himself to shake his head. "No . . . when I'm not working, I want to spend my time with you." This was the right thing to have said. Lisa turned to English, "I'm insisting that he plays. I'm sure you're right. It will do him good."

So it was agreed that Harry should play golf with Jack English every Sunday morning. When they met for the first time at the club house, English said, "Listen, pal. I'm not playing. You're my alibi. I've got a hot piece of tail I want to take care of. You get it?" Startled, Harry said, "So what do I do?" English grinned. "You can get fixed up with a foursome. Be a pal. I'll do the same for you any time you want." So Harry played foursomes while English had a couple of hours in the hay with his girl-friend. Then Harry began to see there was a chance for him to cheat if he found the right girl.

Then one evening when he returned from the office, Lisa herself gave him what he was hoping for . . . Lisa herself . . .

CHAPTER FOUR

Harry had a depressing day in the office. Nothing had gone right. He knew that if he had been a more forceful salesman he would have got a rich client from Texas on the dotted line, but at the last moment, the tall, leathery-looking man had shaken his head and said he wanted more time to think before he committed himself. The deal that slipped through Harry's fingers was worth three hundred thousand dollars.

Feeling deflated, he drove home and walked out on to the terrace where Lisa was sitting in her wheelchair. She was staring across the magnificent garden where three Chinese gardeners were looking busy and doing nothing. One glance at her sullen expression made Harry's heart sink. She was obviously in one of her bad moods.

As he came over to kiss her, she waved him away.

"Don't touch me!"

Harry sighed and sat down near her.

"Had a bad day, darling?"

"When don't I? That woman Selby is a fool! I'm thinking of getting rid of her!"

Remembering Miss Selby's glacial smile this news was no skin off Harry's nose.

"You know best . . . I've never thought much of her."

This was quite the wrong thing to have said.

"She has more brains in her little finger than you have in your head!" Lisa snapped viciously.

To-To, a small, sharp-eyed Japanese, came out on to the terrace with a dry martini which he placed on the table by Harry, bowed and withdrew.

"And you drink too much!" Lisa looked enviously at the ice-beaded glass. Dr Gourley wouldn't allow her to drink any alcohol and Lisa liked a drink.

"I'm sorry," Harry said. "This happens to be my first drink of the day. Would you rather I didn't have it?"

"Oh, have it!" Lisa bit her thin underlip. "I want to be taken out tonight."

"Why, sure. Where shall we go? The Yacht Club? Bernini? Alfredo?"

"I'm sick of those places. We'll go to the Saigon Restaurant."

Harry was surprised.

Along the waterfront there was a number of small, somewhat crummy restaurants and bars. When he worked at the store, he often went to them. He knew the Saigon Restaurant, but had never eaten there. He didn't fancy Vietnamese food. This restaurant was shabby, and usually full of tourists after a cheap meal, and the idea of Lisa dining there seemed to him to be a mistake.

"Do you think you'll like it? It's always crammed with tourists."

"That's where we are going!"

"Well, fine . . . I'll call them to book a table."

So they went. It was always a commotion to get Lisa from her wheelchair into the Aston Martin. Harry had to lift her out of the chair and into the bucket seat. She always complained that he was hurting her. Then he had to collapse the chair and stow it in the back of the car.

They drove down to the crowded waterfront, arriving at the restaurant around nine o'clock. He wheeled her into the big, rather dingy main dining hall.

Dong Tho, the owner of the restaurant, came scurrying forward. Harry had alerted him on the telephone who Lisa was. A tubby little man with a yellow wrinkled skin and bright black eyes, wearing the traditional black Vietnamese dress, Dong Tho bowed to the ground and smiled as he led them into a private room, away from the main restaurant and that overlooked the busy harbour. There were carnations on the table, and it was obvious from the snow white tablecloth and the way the table had been set that Dong Tho had made special efforts to please, but Lisa wasn't impressed.

"I expect we will be poisoned," she said as Harry wheeled her chair up to the table.

Dong Tho giggled with embarrassment. He handed out two menus, a foot long. Harry stared at the list of dishes: they meant nothing to him, then he looked at Lisa.

"Should we leave it to him?"

"I suppose so," Lisa said indifferently. Harry could see that she was now sorry to have come, but since it had been her idea, she couldn't take it out on him. "This is a mistake."

Harry could have slapped her. He was embarrassed for the little man hovering around them. He told him they wanted a simple Vietnamese meal and would he arrange it?

While they waited, Lisa stared out of the window, watching the crowds milling around the sponge fishing boats that had just come in. She wasn't in the mood for light conversation so Harry kept quiet. Then the door opened and a girl came in carrying a tray with the first of Dong Tho's offerings. The girl was wearing Vietnamese costume: white silk trousers and a sheath long tunic of rose pink. Her hair was plaited and lay in a thick black rope down her slim back: the sign of virginity: the married Vietnamese women wear their hair up.

She came into the room behind Lisa and facing Harry. He looked at her, then his heart skipped a beat. He had never seen any woman quite so beautiful. The small, delicate features, the big, almond-shaped eyes, the fairy-like figure rocked him back on his mental heels. He quickly looked away as the girl began to place the dishes before them.

Lisa glanced at her, then seeing her beauty, looked sharply at Harry, but Harry had somehow managed to hoist a bored expression on his face and was now looking at the dishes.

"This looks acceptable," he said. "What do you think?"

"I suppose so."

The girl had gone. Harry had a feeling that the sun had shone on him – a white, burning, bone-melting sun – for the space of a few seconds and now he was in sudden gloom.

The girl was Dong Tho's daughter. She was eighteen years of age. Her mother, an American, once worked at the American Embassy in Saigon. She had met and married Dong Tho and had one child: Tania. They had left Saigon when Tania was five years of age and had settled in Paradise City. Dong Tho had opened his restaurant with his wife's money. When Tania was sixteen years of age, her mother died. She had been eaten up with cancer for some years: her death came as no surprise.

Tania had to take her place. She worked in the restaurant, hating it. With half-American, half-Vietnamese blood, she found the need to balance her life correctly bewildering.

When she came in to change the dishes and to bring more dishes, Harry again gave her a quick appraisal, careful it was quick because he was aware of Lisa's hostility towards the girl.

This fairy-like beauty caught at his throat. She had all the advantages of Vietnamese beauty, but retained the American feminine figure. Her breasts made a blood stirring mound under her rose pink tunic, her legs were long and her hips narrow, but solid.

Lisa found fault with everything although she ate well. Harry was glad when the meal finally ended.

"That girl ... " Lisa said as they waited for the check. "She's a half-caste. What do you think of her?"

"Is she? I didn't notice." Harry looked out of the window. "Anyway, I'm not interested in Orientals."

Lisa leaned forward, her eyes glittering.

"What are you interested in, Harry?"

He forced a smile.

"I'll tell you," he lied. "I'm interested in you. I remember when we first met ... when it was never better. I go along with that memory, darling ... the best ever."

Lisa's hard, sad face crumpled a little. She put her hand on his.

"That's the nicest, loveliest thing you have ever said to me, Harry."

For the next three days, Harry dreamed of Tania. Then the following morning when he was in his office, Miss Bernstein came in to tell him the client who had a luncheon date with him had had to cancel.

Harry saw his chance.

"Too bad ... well, phone the Yacht Club I'm not coming."

Miss Bernstein looked suspiciously at him.

"Where will you be lunching, Mr Lewis?"

"I don't know ... I'll get a sandwich somewhere."

Harry went to the Saigon Restaurant. As soon as Dong Tho saw him, he bowed to the ground and conducted him to the private room.

A minute later, Tania came in with the menu. They looked at each other. Harry knew he couldn't afford to waste time. He smiled his charming smile and said, "You're the most beautiful woman I have ever seen."

There was that Oriental, blank expression on her face that was to bother Harry for months ahead.

"Thank you,' she said and handed him the menu.

Her closeness, the fairy-like slimness of her, her ivory, perfect skin set Harry on fire.

"What is your name?" he asked.

"Tania."

"I am Harry Lewis."

"Yes."

Tania knew all about Harry Lewis, and especially all

about Mrs Harry Lewis who was said to be the richest woman in Paradise City.

Harry hesitated. He knew he might not have the opportunity to visit the restaurant again for weeks. He had to rush his fences. There was something about the way the girl was looking at him that encouraged him.

"Have you anything to do next Sunday morning?" he asked. This was kill or cure. He knew the approach was crude, but he had no alternative.

There was no change of expression. She continued to regard him with that Oriental, deadpan face.

"I have to be here at midday."

"But before then . . . you aren't tied up?"

"No."

Harry drew in a deep breath. He said gently, "Could we meet somewhere? I would like to talk to you . . . to get to know you better."

She lowered her eyes. She looked so lovely Harry had to restrain himself from shoving away the table and taking her in his arms.

"I must ask my father," she said quietly, not looking at him.

Harry thought: God! Now, what have I started?

"Do you have to?" he asked, alarmed.

She looked at him and smiled reassuringly.

"My father has great admiration for Americans. He is very understanding. What would you like to eat?"

"Oh . . . " Harry relaxed. "To eat? Oh, anything . . . I'm not hungry."

She nodded and went away.

Harry lit a cigarette and stared out of the window. Was he walking into trouble? Dealing with Orientals might be tricky, and yet . . . he thought of that slim body, that exquisite body.

Tania found Dong Tho supervising in the kitchen.

"Papa . . . " She beckoned.

He followed her out into the corridor.

"Mr Lewis wants to talk to me on Sunday morning," she said. "Where can I take him?"

Dong Tho's little black eyes lit up with joy.

"Ask him here, of course. He can always have the private room."

Tania looked steadily at her father, then shook her head.

"There should be a bed, Papa."

Dong Tho flinched, but he was a realist. His brain always worked swiftly. If his daughter became the mistress of the husband of the richest woman in the City, not only Tania, but he, himself, must surely benefit.

"There's the Wang-Cho Hotel," he suggested. "It is very discreet."

Tania shook her head.

"Oh no. Mr Lewis wouldn't like that. He is a great gentleman. The rooms are too small and there is only the bed. No, that wouldn't do." She paused, then looked steadily at her father. "I believe he has fallen in love with me."

Dong Tho brightened. This was becoming better and better. He thought for a long moment, selecting and discarding, then he said, "I could speak to Anna Woo. She might let you have her apartment for the morning."

Anna Woo was the most successful call-girl in the Chinese quarter of the City. She had a luxurious one-room apartment on the ground floor of an apartment block inhabited by rich Chinese who minded their own business and were never curious.

"That would do very well," Tania said.

"But Anna is a great thief." Dong Tho frowned. "It will cost a lot of my money. Are you sure he is serious? This isn't just a one-night stand?"

"No ... I am sure he is very serious."

"Then I will telephone her now."

Tania went into the kitchen and filled a bowl with Chinese soup. She filled another bowl with fried shrimps and rice and carried them to Harry.

"Well?" he asked feverishly. "Have you spoken to your father?"

"Not yet," Tania said, putting the bowls before him. "Please enjoy your lunch." As she left the room, she paused and looked at him, then she smiled. "Don't be anxious," and she shut the door.

"Well, that's how it began," Al Barney said, accepting another cigarette. "It had to end in trouble, of course, but these sort of affairs generally do, but the following Sunday morning was the happiest Harry had ever spent, and after all those months of living like a monk, he became obsessed with Tania."

As luck would have it, Lisa was having one of her bad spells. From time to time, she had a lot of pain and when Harry went to her room this Sunday morning, Helgar met him at the door and said Madame shouldn't be disturbed. She was under sedation. This was a relief to Harry as he was so worked up at the thought of meeting Tania, he wasn't too sure that he wouldn't have betrayed himself if Lisa had seen him. He told Helgar he would be back in a couple of hours or so, and she stared at him with her cold, hostile eyes, saying nothing.

Harry had already called Jack English, warning him he would not be at the club house. English said it was okay with him because his girl had the "curse" and he would be playing golf.

"Found something interesting, Harry?"

"Yes. We'll have to take it in turns now."

"My luck! Well, okay, you've been a pal to me. I'll go along with you."

Harry was pleased with Anna Woo's apartment. There was parking space under cover for the Aston Martin, and when Tania let him into the apartment, he was startled at the luxury of it all. Anna Woo knew how to live. The big airy room with its green sun shutters, its ornate furniture and blood-red, heavy pile carpet and its king's size divan made an ideal love-nest.

Tania was wearing a pale blue sheath over her white trousers and she had her hair loose . . . it reached down to her waist. She looked so lovely that Harry could only stand and stare at her.

"Would you like a drink first, Harry?" she asked, smiling at him. "Or shall we make love now?"

They made love at first violently and then gently and tenderly. They made love like this three times before Harry realised he had been in the apartment over three hours.

"My God! I must go!"

While he was dressing Tania lay like an ivory goddess, naked on the divan, watching him. She was smiling gently, although her heart was beating fast. Had she made a mistake? Was this just this once and now satisfied, the American would forget her, but she need not have worried.

"How about next Sunday?" Harry asked as he slipped on his sports shirt.

She got off the bed, shaking her head. Her heart beat less fast.

"My friend won't be able to let me have this apartment again . . . it was a special favour."

Harry stared at her in dismay as she began to dress.

"But we must . . . isn't there any other place you know where we could go?"

For the past two days both she and Dong Tho had hunted for some other place. Dong Tho had been horrified at Anna Woo's charges.

"There is a small furnished apartment – not quite as good as this – but nice, that is to let opposite," Tania said. It was in fact Anna Woo who had told her about it. "It costs one hundred dollars a month . . . three months in advance."

Harry didn't hesitate.

"Take it," he said. "I'll give you the money." He thought a little uneasily of his dwindling bank account. He would have to try to cut down on his personal spending.

He gave her three one hundred dollar bills. "I must go," He took her in his arms, fondled and kissed her, then knowing he was dangerously late back home, he said good-bye. "The next Sunday at nine o'clock . . . across the way."

She smiled happily.

"Yes."

Harry met Jack English at the Yacht Club. Both of them had been lunching clients.

"I won't be at the Golf Club on Sunday," Harry said.

"Oh, come on!" English looked dismayed. "We agreed to take it in turns. It's my Sunday."

"I'm sorry."

English's eyes narrowed.

"You could be. If you don't cover me – I don't cover you."

Harry had anticipated that this would be English's reaction. He had given the situation some thought.

"Do you think we could fix something with Joe Gates?"

Joe Gates was the Golf Club's barman who handled all the telephone messages coming in for members out on the course.

English brightened.

"That's an idea . . . how?"

"Why don't we slip him twenty bucks a week, and if either of our wives call, he can say we are out of reach. Before we leave our girl-friends, we call him and he alerts us if there have been any messages."

English regarded Harry with admiration.

"What a mind! that's terrific! For twenty bucks Joe would betray his own mother. Okay, leave it to me. I'll talk to him. You pay him one week . . . I'll pay him the other. Okay?"

Later, English called Harry at the office and said it was fixed. Harry had already warned him Miss Bernstein listened in, so English just said, "Joe has arranged our game for Sunday. It's in the bag."

Somehow, Harry got through the days while waiting for Sunday. He could only think of Tania, and once or twice the far-away expression made Lisa demand sharply what he was thinking about. Startled, Harry said he was wondering how he could persuade the Texan – his name was Hal Garrard – to buy that parcel of land.

"I am sure I can sell him if only I can find the right approach."

"Is that all you're thinking about?"

"Well, damn it! It's worth three hundred thousand." Harry lit a cigarette so he needn't meet her eyes. "It's a big deal."

Lisa shrugged.

"You men ... we have all the money we want. You're just greedy."

Harry thought grimly that she had all the money she wanted, but he hadn't.

"Look, darling," he said quietly, "it's all very well for you to talk that way. I have only twenty thousand, and it gets used up with so many incidental expenses."

She regarded him, her hard, pain-worn face suspicious.

"If you want any more money, tell me. Give me your bills ... I'll pay them."

Harry controlled an outburst with an effort.

"That makes me a bit of a gigolo, doesn't it?"

She lifted her black eyebrows. Well, you are, aren't you? her expression conveyed.

"It's my money, Harry. Will you please turn on the TV?"

Well, that was that. Somehow Harry told himself he would have to make do with his twenty thousand. At least, he could now charge his clothes to Lisa's account, but he would have to be very careful. He mustn't give her the excuse to ask to see his Bank pass sheets, and this was something she might well do.

Saturday night, he got a shock.

They were sitting on the terrace after dinner. Harry was trying to read a thriller which didn't hold his interest as his mind was on Tania and thinking that in another few hours he would be lying in her arms when Lisa who had been doing a crossword puzzle said, "I forgot to tell you, Harry. We are going to Miami tomorrow morning. The Van Johnsons have invited us to lunch."

Harry nearly gave himself away. With an effort, he kept his face expressionless.

"I'm sorry, darling, I can't go. I promised Jack ... "

"We are going, Harry!"

"Look, why not let To-To drive you. I have a foursome with Jack and ... "

"You are driving me, Harry," Lisa said in that cold, flat voice that brooked no argument. "You have been invited."

"But look ... " Harry began, then seeing Lisa turn pale and her eyes light up with fury, he stopped short. He couldn't face the scene that was bound to come if he persisted in this. "Well, okay ... I'll call Jack," and getting to his feet, he went into the lounge. He stood for a long moment, so furious at his own cowardice, so frustrated that he now couldn't make love to Tania after all the past days of waiting and dreaming, he wanted to go back on the terrace and kill this hook-nosed, cripple bitch, but he controlled himself. He dare not telephone Tania. Either Helgar or To-To could listen in from one of the many telephone extensions in the house. So he called English. He said he was taking Lisa to Miami and he was sorry he would have to scrub the game. English was quick to realise what had happened. He said it was bad luck. Maybe the following Sunday.

There was no way to get word to Tania. The telephone was too dangerous. The Post Office was three miles away. He scarcely slept that night.

They left in the Rolls soon after ten o'clock the following morning. As he drove, Harry thought of Tania

84

waiting for him, thinking he had betrayed her. Somehow, he must control himself.

Lisa said abruptly, "I don't know what's the matter with you this morning. You act like a stuffed dummy. Haven't you anything to say to me?"

Well, there were other Sundays, Harry thought. He was behaving stupidly. He just couldn't afford to take any risks.

"Sorry," he said. "I've got this deal on my mind." Then he began to make that small talk which was so vapid, Lisa told him to stop it.

"If you're so disinterested in me that you can't think of anything better to talk about than this, then for God's sake, keep quiet!"

They got back from Miami soon after five o'clock. On the way back Lisa criticised the Van Johnsons, the meal and their servants.

To keep her happy, Harry agreed with everything she said. When they got home, Lisa said, "I'm tired. I'll take a bath. We'll have a light supper on the terrace."

"Okay," Harry said. "You take a rest. I'll run the car down to Jefferson's. The carburettors want retuning. Did you notice how she was running on the way back?"

"She was running perfectly," Lisa said, staring suspiciously at him.

"I was driving," Harry said quietly. "She's using too much gas. I want to get it fixed."

"Oh, very well."

When he had carried her to her chair and had seen Helgar wheel her into the house, Harry got back into the Rolls and drove fast to the nearest drug store, some two miles down the long avenue. He parked the car and shut himself into a telephone booth.

He called the Saigon Restaurant.

Dong Tho answered.

"Is Tania there?"

When Dong Tho recognised Harry's voice, he drew in a long sigh of relief. Both he and Tania had been distracted all day, believing that Harry had had his fun and the affair was over. Although they were three hundred dollars in credit, they were now landed with six months' lease on the apartment as well as Anna Woo's exorbitant charge for the loan of her apartment.

"A moment, please, sir."

Dong Tho got Tania to the telephone. When he told her Harry was on the line, she pressed her hands to her full breasts and closed her eyes. Dong Tho gave her a sharp slap.

"Talk to him!"

"Tania?"

"Yes."

"This is Harry."

"Yes."

"Tania, listen . . . I had to go to Miami with my wife. I couldn't contact you. It has driven me half out of my mind. I am very sorry. Will you forgive me?"

Tania smiled, her eyes closed.

"I understand. It is very difficult for you. I am very sorry too."

Harry wiped the sweat from his forehead with the back of his hand.

"You're not angry with me?"

"Angry with you? I love you."

Those words: *I love you* kept Harry walking on air for the rest of the week. It was a bad week for Lisa who remained in bed, suffering. Harry saw little of her, but he dare not leave the house once he had returned from the office. He waited and longed for Sunday to come. He told himself that if Lisa prevented him from seeing Tania this Sunday, he would tell her to go to hell – knowing that he wouldn't.

But it was Lisa who told him he should play golf with English on Sunday.

The apartment Tania had rented wasn't anything like so deluxe as Anna Woo's love nest, but Harry liked it better.

It was simpler, more homely, and there was a king's size bed, and that was the only thing Harry really cared about.

"This time," Tania said as she slid out of her clothes, "I make love to you. You are passive ... I am active. It is the way the East make love sometimes."

She made him lie flat on the bed.

"You must keep your eyes open. We must look at each other."

The next five minutes were the most exciting and exotic moments in Harry's life.

Later, as they lay side by side, she said, "I have an idea how we can meet more often. You want us to meet more often, don't you, Harry?"

Harry pulled her closer to him.

"Of course I do, but I don't see how. I've been battering my brains out how it can be done, but I can't see how. I have to be damned careful, Tania ... you don't know how careful."

"Yes, I do." She raised her exquisite face and looked at him. "Suppose she did find out ... what would happen?"

Harry flinched at the very thought.

"She would divorce me, and that would be that."

"What does that mean, please?"

"I would have to find a job."

"But you have a good job, haven't you, Harry?"

"Not really. She could throw me out. The business belongs to her – everything belongs to her. If she divorced me, I wouldn't have a cent."

Tania absorbed this information, her face expressionless.

"I see ... then you must be very careful," she said finally. "But couldn't you visit me sometimes when she has gone to bed? What time does she go to bed?"

"Always at ten-thirty unless we have guests. But I don't see how I can. I couldn't take the car out. Someone would hear it."

"But suppose I was waiting for you in a car? I could drive you here and take you back."

Harry was startled. This could be an idea.

"Can you drive?"

"Of course."

"Have you a car?"

"No, but we could buy one. I know of a very cheap, good car that is for sale. It is only four hundred dollars . . . secondhand."

Right at this moment Harry had only eight hundred dollars in his account to last him another fifteen days before his allowance was paid in. He moved uneasily.

"I'll have to think about it, Tania."

Tania was longing to own a car. She saw his hesitation. Her father always said if something was worth while, you had to fight for it.

"If we are going to buy this car, we have to do it quickly," she said, a determined note in her voice. "The owner of the car is Papa's friend. He warned me if I don't make up my mind by tomorrow, he will have to sell the car to another friend."

Harry was thinking. His bedroom was near the patio. It would be simple and safe to leave by the patio door and walk down the drive without being seen. Ever since Lisa's accident she had gone to bed at ten-thirty unless there had been a party. He had gone to his room to read in bed. Lisa always took sleeping pills. She slept through until seven o'clock. Yes, this could be safe. He could leave the house around eleven-thirty, spend a couple of hours with Tania, get back and no one would be the wiser.

But four hundred dollars!

Seeing he was still hesitating, Tania said wistfully, "But perhaps it is too expensive? Perhaps you prefer to see me only on Sunday?"

That decided Harry. He pulled her to him, his hand running down her slim, beautiful back.

"Buy the car . . . I'll give you a cheque."

She pressed her body against his.

"Wouldn't cash be safer?"

"Yes, you're right. I'll send the money by registered mail."

"Then when you can see me, you have only to telephone."

"I can't do that . . . they listen in."

"But you can. If you dial the restaurant, you can say you have the wrong number. Papa always answers the phone. He knows your voice. Then he will tell me and I will be waiting in the car."

Harry regarded her thoughtfully.

"You've really thought this out, haven't you?"

"It's because I love you and I realise how careful you have to be."

Harry rolled her on her back.

"Now, you're going to be passive and I am going to be very active."

Before he left the apartment, he telephoned the Golf Club. Joe Gates said with a chuckle there had been no messages.

On his way home, Harry wondered how to raise $400 without crippling his account. He had the uneasy feeling that he was getting into a network of lies and intrigues, but he didn't care. As he drove into the garage, he deliberately steered the Aston Martin into the concrete post that separated one garage from the other. He smashed the front offside wing and the headlamp.

"What's the matter with you?" Lisa demanded shrilly when he told her of the accident. "Are you drunk?"

"Well, it's done," Harry said, shrugging. "I'm sorry . . . accidents will happen. I'd better take it down to Jefferson's. He'll fix it.

Jefferson, the owner of the garage, liked Harry. They talked the same language about cars and Harry knew Jefferson had no time for Lisa. After Jefferson had examined the damage, he said he could fix it for ninety dollars.

"Do me a favour?" Harry said. "Will you pad the bill out

to four hundred and ninety?" He winked. "I'll pick up the four hundred when Mrs Lewis pays. Okay?"

Jefferson grinned.

"Sure. It's a pleasure to do anything for you, Mr Lewis. Let's see: wing straightened and repainted, new head-lamp, hubcap replaced, front axle taken down and straightened, brakes readjusted. Yeah ... can do."

When the bill came in, Lisa raised the roof. Harry said humbly that an accident was an accident and the insurance would take care of it, but Jefferson would be obliged to have a cheque right away. Lisa wrote the cheque and threw it at him.

"Be more careful in the future!"

So without knowing it, Lisa paid for Tania's car.

Tania's plan worked. When Harry felt the urge, he would call the restaurant, apologise for dialling the wrong number. Around eleven-thirty p.m. when To-To had gone to bed and Helgar was in her room watching TV, Harry sneaked out of his bedroom, locked the door, left by the patio door which he locked after him, then went silently down the drive to where Tania was waiting in her T.R.4 at the corner of the road.

Now life for Harry became an agony of nerves and an ecstasy of the flesh. But he was now too committed to draw back. The more he saw of Tania the more he desired her. She seldom asked him for money, and then only to buy some little thing that was of no consequence. He realised that this erotic and wonderful love affair was costing him very little. After three months of this, Tania reminded him that the rent was due, and again he had to think how he could get Lisa to pay the three hundred dollars.

Lisa had just had her bedroom redecorated. Harry went along to the blond homo decorator who he knew hated Lisa and talked him into adding four hundred dollars to his bill: three for Harry and one for himself. The homo had a tricky moment convincing Lisa why the price had gone over the original estimate, but as she was very satisfied with her room, she grudgingly paid. So again she paid for Harry's affair.

One Sunday morning as Tania and Harry were lying on the divan after their love-making, Tania said, "Please tell me about the Esmaldi diamonds."

"How do you know about them?" Harry asked, surprised. He was relaxed and feeling sleepy.

"I have read about the necklace. Is it very beautiful?"

"I guess so ... yes, it is."

"Does she wear it often?"

"Scarcely at all. It stays in the safe. It's a damn shame really, she hasn't the looks to wear it. On a beautiful woman, it would look magnificent."

Tania edged closer to him.

"Would it look nice on me?"

Harry raised his head and surveyed her naked body. He smiled, nodding.

"More than magnificent."

"If anything happened to her would you have the necklace, Harry?"

"Not a chance. She has left it to a museum, and besides, nothing is going to happen to her."

Tania's almond-shaped eyes opened wide.

"To a museum?"

"That's right. The Fine Arts Museum in Washington."

"So no other woman will ever wear it once she is dead?"

"That's right."

Tania drew in a long slow breath.

"I think that is very selfish."

"Yes, but there it is ... it's her necklace."

Lisa had had a bad week of pain. Her temper became insufferable. Even Helgar came under her lash, but Harry suffered most. He was in the lounge, nervously pacing up and down, when Dr Gourley who had been giving Lisa a check-up came into the room.

Dr Gourley was a tall, thin, distinguished-looking man who Harry liked.

"How did you find her, Doctor?" Harry asked anxiously.

"Nothing to worry about," Gourley said. "She is bound to have pain from time to time. I've changed her drugs. She'll settle down in a day or two." He too had had the sharp edge of Lisa's tongue, but as she was one of his most profitable patients, he accepted her insults.

"She's not in danger?"

"Danger?" Gourley smiled and shook his head. "She'll last for years. She has a splendid heart. No ... you don't have to worry about that, but she does need a change. I've advised her to take a few weeks off in the yacht. Nothing better for her than to have some sea air and a change of background."

When the doctor had gone, Harry went up to Lisa's room. He found her in bed, her hard, pinched face pale and her mouth a thin line of pain.

"That fool thinks I should have a sea trip," she said as Harry shut the bedroom door. "We will go to the Bahamas. Tell Captain Ainsworth. We'll leave at the end of the week. We'll go for six weeks. I've already called the Van Johnsons. They will be coming with us."

Harry was appalled. He thought of Tania. To be away from her for six weeks! To be cooped up on that damned yacht with those awful Van Johnson bores!

"But, darling, I can't be away from the office for six weeks," he protested, trying to smile.

She stared at him, her black eyes glittering.

"Don't talk nonsense! Of course you can! Miss Bernstein can handle the office far better than you! Tell Captain Ainsworth!"

Harry spent most of the day in the office trying to find a way out. After lunch, he called the Saigon Restaurant from the Yacht Club and asked to speak to Tania.

"I must see you tonight."

"Harry, dear, I'm sorry, but I have my monthly thing."

"It doesn't matter. I must see you."

That night when Lisa had gone to bed, Harry met Tania at the corner of the street.

"No, we won't go to the apartment," he said, sitting beside her in the little car. "Just listen . . . this is important . . ."

He told her he had to go with Lisa to the Bahamas and they would be away for six weeks. Tania caught her breath in anguish.

"But don't worry, it's not going to be six weeks for me." Harry said, holding her hand. "I want you to send a telegram to the yacht on September 3rd." He took from his wallet a folded sheet of paper. "The address and the message is written down here. I shall be back by the 4th and we can have three whole days and nights together before I have to return to the yacht."

Two weeks later while the yacht was at anchor in the harbour of Andros Island before making the crossing of the Exuma Sound to Nassau, the telegram arrived.

Harry had had a gruesome fourteen days. At least, Lisa had been in a better mood but being cooped up with the Van Johnsons had nearly driven him crazy. The four of them were sitting in the sun, drinking midday cocktails, when one of the crew came up to Harry with the telegram. Harry was aware that Lisa was watching him while he read it. Then he passed it over to her.

Golden Arrow Yacht
Andros Island.
Have had second thoughts. Please meet on site on 5th.

Hal Garrard.

Lisa stared suspiciously at him.

"What does this mean?"

"He's the guy I nearly sold. The Texan who's been after

that parcel of land," Harry explained. "It's a three hundred thousand deal, Lisa."

"How did he know where to contact you?"

"I've never ceased to contact him."

"Well, Miss Bernstein can handle it."

"No ... he hates the sight of her. I'll have to go back."

Sam Van Johnson, a big, puffy, balding man, helped him.

"For Pete's sake, Harry! Three hundred thousand! Boy! That's money! How will you get back?"

Harry was still looking directly at Lisa who was glaring angrily at the telegram.

"Your father wanted to sell this land, darling," he said quietly, aware his heart was thumping. "Do you want me to go or don't you?"

"Oh, go! But it doesn't mean he will buy!" Lisa looked at him. "Where will you stay?"

"Oh, some motel. I doubt if I'll get into the Majestic. It's bound to be full."

"So I won't know where you are?"

"But, darling, I'll be on the site most of the time."

"I can't contact you there."

"I'll keep in touch, and I'll meet you at Nassau."

Harry flew back to Paradise City. An hour after arriving, he was with Tania in her apartment.

Their love-making was long, tender and passionate. Knowing they dare not be seen together in the City, Tania had arranged for meals to be sent in. The meals arrived from the Saigon restaurant, brought by a smiling Vietnamese waiter.

This suited Harry. He was enchanted with Tania and when he wasn't making physical love with her, he liked nothing better than to lie on the divan and watch her move around the room, prepare his meals or sit on the floor while she talked to him.

On the morning of the second day together, she said suddenly, "Harry ... I would so very much like to see your home. It is your chance to show it to me. Will you?"

The house had been shut up. Helgar was on the yacht. To-To and the rest of the staff had gone off for their annual holiday. The elaborate burglar alarms, wired direct to police headquarters, satisfied Lisa the house was safe to be left unoccupied.

Tania's request startled Harry.

"I'm afraid not. That's taking too big a risk. My God! If Lisa ... "

"But couldn't we go late tonight? No one would know. I do so want to see your home."

But the thought scared Harry.

"I'm sorry ... no, Tania."

When you want anything, you have to fight for it, Dong Tho had said so often to her.

"All right then!" For the first time since he had known her, her beautiful little face became set and hard. "I have done so much for you. I give myself to you whenever you want me. I had hoped you would have done something for me."

Harry hesitated. From her expression he guessed she would now sulk for the rest of the evening if not for his remaining day, and time was running out.

"All right, we'll go."

She gave a squeal of delight and threw herself in his arms.

Soon after midnight, he led her up the drive and around to the patio door. Here, he turned off the concealed switch that disconnected the burglar alarm.

"What are you going, Harry?"

"Turning the switch off. If I didn't, we would have a lot of policemen here in three minutes. The whole house is wired direct to the police headquarters. By turning this switch, the alarm is cut off."

He groped under a flower pot containing yellow begonias and took from under it the key to the patio door.

"I always leave it here," he explained as he unlocked the door. "If I lost it and couldn't get back to my bedroom after seeing you, I'd be sunk."

He led her into the house.

The shutters were closed and the curtains drawn. It was safe to turn on the lights.

She walked with him through the rooms. She stood for nearly three minutes staring at the fitted kitchen, her almond-shaped eyes wide. The bathrooms fascinated her. Harry had now got over his scare and was enjoying seeing her utter bewilderment at such luxury.

"But those taps are solid gold!" she exclaimed, staring at Lisa's bath.

"That's right," Harry said. "All the fittings in here are gold."

"But how can one be so rich!"

"Lisa just is."

She stood in the doorway of the enormous lounge, her hands against her breasts. Watching her in her white trousers and her pale blue tunic, Harry thought how lovely she looked. She examined everything, but touched nothing. She stared at the fully-equipped bar, the big colour TV set, the stereo radiogram and the rack of L.P. records, the furniture, the decor and the hangings. She moved as if she were in a dream.

"All this belongs to you, Harry?"

"Nothing belongs to me . . . I just live here."

He showed her his bedroom.

"And you sleep in this beautiful room all alone?"

"Yes, but I dream of you."

She looked at him, smiling.

"Do you . . . really?"

"Really . . . come on, let's go."

Her black eyes became appealing.

"Please, Harry, may I see the Esmaldi necklace?"

Harry hesitated. Then seeing the longing expression in her eyes, he hadn't the heart to refuse.

He took her into Lisa's bedroom. Tania caught her

breath as he switched on the lights. The room was the acme of luxury, comfort and taste. The beauty and magnificence of it still impressed Harry.

"But this is truly wonderland," Tania whispered, moving into the room. "It's the most beautiful room I have ever seen."

"Isn't it!"

Harry went over to one of the hidden buttons concealed under the edge of Lisa's dressing-table.

"What are you doing?" Tania asked curiosly, joining him.

"Opening the safe. There are two buttons: one here ... the other across the room. This one cuts the alarm. The other opens the safe." He crossed the room and located the second button cunningly hidden in the ornate woodwork that surrounded the radiator. As he pressed the button, the safe door, set in the wall, slid open.

"But that's wonderful! Oh, Harry, please let me do it! Please!"

So Harry reclosed the safe and let her touch the first button and then the second. She clapped her hands like an excited child as the door of the safe slid open.

"Oh, to be able to live like this!" she exclaimed. "This is the most wonderful night of my life!"

"Wait," Harry said. He was now getting a big bang out of her excitement. He reached into the safe and took out a long, flat jewel case. "Take your clothes off, Tania."

She stared at him.

"I don't understand."

"Go on ... take them off."

With trembling fingers, she slid out of her clothes and stood before him. He opened the case and drew out the Esmaldi necklace that glittered like three ropes of stars.

"Don't move," he went on as Tania gasped at the sight of the diamonds.

He fastened the necklace around her slim throat, then moved her to the full length mirror and stood away. Her

97

ivory, satin-smooth skin was the perfect background for the three strands of glittering diamonds.

She stood hypnotised, staring at her reflection.

"I knew it," Harry said a little huskily. "They were created for you."

She said nothing. She looked and she looked and she looked. After she had remained motionless for some five minutes, Harry gently undid the clasp and returned the necklace to its case.

"And no one will ever wear them but her?" Tania said quietly as she dressed.

"That's right. They'll be behind armoured glass in a museum."

Tania was strangely quiet as they drove back to the little apartment. She looked around the small, simply furnished room as she entered, her face expressionless.

"What it is to have money, Harry," she said, then she shrugged and smiled. "Now let us make beautiful love."

For the first time since they had lain together, Harry had an uneasy idea that Tania wasn't with him. He felt her thoughts were far away.

The following day, he had to catch the eleven-forty plane to Nassau. They woke late and while he was drinking coffee, Tania said suddenly, "Harry ... if anything happened to her, would that wonderful house be yours? Would you have all her money?"

"Yes. When we married, she made a will leaving everything to me, but she will live for years. Her doctor told me."

"Oh," Tania walked her long, slim fingers along the edge of the table. "But one never knows, does one? She could die, then you would be free. Please tell me something truthfully, Harry, if you were free would you want to marry me?"

Harry looked up sharply. Would he? He had never considered marrying Tania. But seeing her beauty and the anxiety in her eyes, he smiled, nodding.

"Of course. But look, darling, she's not going to die for

years and years. She could even outlive me. Let's forget it."

Tania studied him.

"But if you were free, you would really marry me?" Harry felt suddenly uneasy. There was a tension about Tania that was foreign to her.

"Yes, Tania, but I'm not free and I won't be free." He got up from the table. "I must hurry. Time's getting on."

When he had gone, Tania sat on the bed, staring down at her slim hands.

She was thinking of the necklace, the house . . . she also thought of Lisa.

CHAPTER FIVE

Martha, Henry, Gilda and Johnny sat around the table on the terrace and regarded Mrs Lowenstein's jewels. Gilda wanted to try on a ring. She wanted to try on one of the magnificent diamond and gold bracelets, but Martha scooped up the jewels and returned them to the wash-leather bag.

"Here, Henry, you take them," she said and handed the bag across the table to Henry who dropped the bag into his pocket.

Martha sat back and surveyed the other three.

"Now for the second one. Mrs Warren Crail. The take is six hundred and fifty thousand. She leaves on this fishing trip the day after tomorrow. We work the same carpet cleaning gag. We must know who has been left in the house."

Two days later, Gilda, wearing her black wig, her prim dress and sun-goggles, called on the Crails' sumptuous residence. The door was opened by the resident house-keeper, a thin, hard-faced woman who regarded Gilda suspiciously.

Gilda told her story, but she could see this woman wasn't going to be convinced.

"Mrs Crail has said nothing to me about it," the woman said curtly. "Before I let you in, I must have it in writing from Mrs Crail herself," and she shut the door in Gilda's face.

Gilda realised this could be dangerous. The woman had only to look in the telephone book to find the Acme Carpet

100

Cleaning Co. didn't exist. She drove rapidly back to the villa.

Martha listened to her recital, her fat face dark. She looked at Henry.

"What do you think?"

"It's worth the risk," Henry said, gnawing his moustache. "We know where the safe is. These two stand a good chance of breaking in. Yes, I think we should do it tonight. The prize is worth while."

"Who's taking the risk?" Johnny demanded, sitting forward. "Not you! I'm not breaking into a house I know nothing about. No ... we'll let this one cool off and try somewhere else. Let me look at that list."

Henry passed the list over to him and exchanged looks with Martha. Johnny studied the list.

"How about the Lewis's? This diamond necklace? How about grabbing that?" he asked.

"That's out!" Martha snapped.

Johnny stared at her.

"What's the matter with it ... three hundred and fifty grand! That's money!"

Martha had no intention of telling him that the necklace was insured by the National Fidelity and that Maddox of the Claims Department had got her a five year stretch. She kept her prison sentence to herself: only Henry knew about it.

"I tell you it's out ... so it's out!"

Johnny shrugged.

"Don't get worked up. Okay. How about Mrs Alec Johnson? She's on a yacht off Miami according to this. She has four hundred thousand dollars' worth of stuff. Suppose we take a look at her place?"

"I still can't see why we don't do the Crail job," Martha grumbled.

"You do it ... I'm not going to. Let it cool off. How about the Jacksons'?"

"All right, then we'll do that."

This time Gilda had no difficulty in getting into the

house. The caretaker was an old man who had an eye for a pretty girl. He accepted Gilda's story, took her over the house, let her measure the carpet in the main bedroom and gossiped. He told Gilda he was alone in the house and he gave her time to locate the safe and study the window locks.

On her return to the villa, she told them how easy it was. She described the locks on the windows to Johnny who nodded. He then studied the blueprint they had got from Raysons, then grinned.

"It's easy. Okay, we'll do it tonight." He stood up. He was wearing a sweat shirt and swimming trunks. "I'm taking a swim." He went off across the terrace and down to the beach.

Gilda got quickly to her feet and went to her room. In a few moments she reappeared wearing a bikini.

Martha said, "Gilda . . . just a moment."

"What now?" Gilda demanded, pausing and frowning.

"You don't have to be his shadow. You don't have to keep looking at him as if you wanted to eat him. I'm warning you. He's no good. Get him out of your mind."

Gilda flushed scarlet. "Shut your mouth, you old fool!"

"I'm warning you," Martha said, helping herself to a chocolate. "He's no good."

"Oh, go to hell!"

Gilda ran across the terrace and down to the beach.

Martha shrugged her fat shoulders.

"Well, I've warned her."

"And very tactfully too," Henry said dryly. "I'm taking a nap," and he wandered away to his room.

Johnny saw Gilda plunge into the sea and he grinned to himself. He turned on his back and let her reach him.

"Do you think it's going to work tonight?" Gilda asked, treading water.

"Why not?"

"It makes me nervous."

Johnny grimaced, then turned and began to swim towards the beach.

Gilda hesitated, then aware Martha was watching, she swam out to sea.

I am in love with Johnny, she admitted to herself, but that doesn't mean he can use me as he likes. He's ruthless. If I went the whole way with him, he'd drop me. No ... I've got to use my head if I'm to land him and I'm going to! Has he any idea that I'm in love with him? If Martha's spotted it ... has he? She felt a rush of blood to her face.

The second Big Take went off as easily as the first. The whole operation took only fourteen minutes, and they carried away with them four hundred thousand dollars' worth of jewellery.

As they drove back to the villa, Gilda said, "I can't believe it. It's too easy ... so it scares me."

"What's there to be scared about?" Johnny asked impatiently. "That fat old bitch has brains. Her idea is smart. I have to hand it to her. In less than a week we have picked up five hundred thousand dollars' worth of stuff: with little effort and no trouble. The owners don't even know the stuff's gone. The cops don't know we exist. That's smart."

"But we haven't the money," Gilda pointed out. "That's what is worrying me. We couldn't sell the stuff ourselves. It is worthless to us as it is."

Johnny frowned, his eyes narrowing. This hadn't occurred to him.

"You've got something. Okay, we'll do something about that. It's time we had some cash. I'll talk to the Colonel."

They found Martha and Henry waiting anxiously for their return. After the jewels had been examined and put back in the bag, Johnny said, "Let's see Abe tomorrow, Colonel, and get some cash on this lot and the other lot."

Henry looked startled.

"That isn't the arrangement. When we have the Crails' collection, then we see Abe ... and Martha and I see him ... not you and I, Johnny."

Johnny smiled at him. He reached out and picked up the bag, holding it in his big fist as he stared levelly at Henry.

"You and me, Colonel," he said quietly. "Tomorrow."

"Now listen to me ... " Martha began, her face turning purple.

"Quiet!" Johnny said. "I'm talking to the Colonel." He continued to stare at Henry. "I want some money ... not this stuff. I'm not waiting. You and me either go and see Abe tomorrow morning together or I go alone."

Henry knew when he was licked. He knew this powerfully built young man could brush him aside as if he were a fly. Johnny could go to Henry's bedroom, find the other jewels and walk out on them. None of them could stop him.

"All right, Johnny," Henry said mildly. "Then we'll see Abe together tomorrow."

Johnny put the bag of jewels back on the table, nodded, stood up and went to his room.

Martha waited until she heard his bedroom door shut, then looking at Gilda, she said viciously, "Maybe you'd better start loving up this sonofabitch. Someone's got to control him!"

Gilda stared stonily at her, then got up and left them.

"So you think you can handle him!" Martha turned on Henry. "When Abe pays out, that punk will take his share and we'll never get our hands on it!"

Henry stroked his moustache.

"I must think about it."

Martha snorted. She stumped off to bed. She was so furious she forgot to visit the refrigerator and only remembered when she was in bed.

"Oh, the hell with it!" she said to herself and turned off the light.

The following morning, Abe Schulman was sitting at his desk jotting down figures on a sheet of paper. He had had an unsatisfactory week. Although the season was in full swing, nothing of any account had passed through his hands. Police security had been drastically tightened up in Miami and the boys had been scared off. There hadn't been one decent jewel robbery all the week.

He was surprised when Henry and Johnny walked into his office.

"Hello, Colonel ... Johnny ... what brings you here?"

"Money," Johnny said, putting a brief-case on the desk. Abe smiled bitterly.

"Who doesn't want money?" His little eyes rested on the brief-case. "You got something for me?"

"Yeah."

"Wait." Abe got up and locked the office door.

Johnny unzipped the case, took from it three small wash-leather bags and a parcel done up in tissue paper. He undid the tape around the bags and poured the contents of the bags in separate piles on Abe's blotter. At the sight of the diamonds, emeralds and rubies and four splendid ropes of pearls Abe sucked in his breath. This was the finest haul he had seen in years.

"The gold, silver and platinum settings are in the parcel, Abe," Henry said.

They waited until Abe examined the various settings, then Johnny said, "The insurance value for this little lot is five hundred and eighty grand."

Abe put on his deadpan expression. He lifted his fat shoulders.

"Never believe insurance values, Johnny, my boy. Quite fatal. Jewellery is always over-insured ... it's a racket."

He spread out the diamonds and breathed over them. He spent ten minutes examining the various stones, regarding the pearl necklaces, now and then screwing a watchmaker's glass in his eye to examine a diamond more closely while Johnny and Henry watched.

Finally, he took the glass from his eye and began to make calculations on a sheet of paper. Then he dropped the pencil and looked at Henry.

"It's good stuff, Colonel ... no doubt about it, but at the present market calculation, I couldn't get more than a hundred and fifty grand. You want a third? We agreed about that ... sheer robbery ... but we agreed and I'm a man of my word. So okay, I pay you fifty thousand dollars." He smiled at Henry. "Right?"

"You can get more for this stuff than that, Abe. Come on, you don't con me," Henry said, shaking his head. "We expected it to go for two hundred thousand."

"No, we don't," Johnny said quietly. "You'll sell this stuff for three hundred and fifty thousand or you don't get it!"

Abe sat back, a pained look of astonishment on his face.

"Are you crazy? Three hundred and fifty? Why I couldn't possibly get two hundred. I know the market."

"So do I," Johnny said. "I've talked to Bernie Baum."

Abe turned puce in the face.

"That thief! Don't make me laugh! Now, listen, Johnny, I know what I'm talking about. I ... "

"Shut up!" Johnny snarled and got to his feet. He leaned across the desk, glaring at Abe. "You pay us a hundred and twenty thousand as our cut or you don't get the stuff. What's it to be?"

Abe eased back in his chair.

"It's impossible, Johnny, but I tell you what I'll do. I'll take a loss. The stuff's good ... I admit that, but the market's lousy. I'll give you eighty thousand. How's that?"

Johnny began to scoop up the diamonds, dropping them into one of the bags. When he began to pick up the emeralds, Abe said, "Now wait a minute ... eighty thousand! It's a fortune! I swear, Johnny, no one would give you more than fifty. I swear it."

Johnny dropped the emeralds into the bag.

"What are you doing?" Abe asked, sweat glistening on his face.

"I'm showing this stuff to Baum," Johnny said, dropping the pearl necklaces into the third bag.

"Now look, Johnny, use your head. Bernie won't give you fifty for them. I know Bernie ... he's a thief." Then as Johnny began to tape the bags, Abe went on hastily, "Okay, I'll give you a hundred thousand. It'll ruin me, but I don't want you to get into Baum's dirty hands ... a hundred thousand."

Johnny paused and looked at him.

"In cash?"

"Of course."

"Right now?"

Abe threw up his hands.

"For God's sake, Johnny, be reasonable. Would I have a hundred grand right here in my office? You'll get the money in cash next week."

"I get it right now or I go to Baum," Johnny said, dropping the bags into the brief-case.

"But I haven't got it!" Abe screamed, banging his fists on the desk. "Listen to me, you sonofabitch ... " which was a mistake.

Johnny reached forward and caught hold of Abe's shirt front. He gave him a little shake, snapping his head back.

"What did you call me?"

Abe wasn't sure if his neck was broken. His fat face turned yellow and his eyes bulged.

"I take it back," he gasped. "I apologise ... "

Johnny released him with a violent shove that nearly sent Abe's chair over backwards.

"I want cash. We'll wait here. Your pals will lend it to you. Go out and raise it!"

"No one will lend me a hundred thousand!" Abe wailed. "You're crazy. I just can't ... "

"Okay ... so you can't ... I'm sick of you," Johnny said. "I'm going to talk to Baum."

Watching all this, Henry realised that Johnny was handling the haggling as he himself never could have handled it. He knew too that Abe would have talked him into accepting the fifty thousand dollar bid.

· Then Abe did something he was to regret. He put his foot on a concealed button under his desk and rang an alarm bell. He always had two strong arm men lolling around in an office down the passage. When dealing with his various clients, Abe never knew when he might need protection and it seemed to him he needed it now.

"Hold it, Johnny. You're a thief, but I'll see what I can do. It'll take time. Suppose you come back, huh? You can leave the stuff in my safe. I can't raise a hundred thousand in five minutes."

"I'll give you three hours, Abe," Johnny said quietly. "We'll wait here."

Abe hesitated, then shrugged, got up and took his hat off a peg.

"Well, okay, I'll see what I can do."

As he unlocked the door, Johnny said, "Abe ... "

Abe paused and turned.

"Now what is it?"

"No tricks."

The two men regarded each other, then Abe forced a smile.

"Of course not, Johnny ... don't be so suspicious. I'll be as quick as I can."

He left the room and they listened to his departing footfalls as he walked down the passage to the elevator.

"Very nice work, Johnny," Henry said. "I couldn't have done it better myself."

Johnny stared indifferently at him.

"You couldn't have done it ... period."

Then the office door swung open and Abe's two thugs moved in swiftly.

The bigger of the two was an immense Negro, standing well over six feet with shoulders like a barn door. His shaven head was glistening with sweat, his flat features were coarse and brutal. Known as Jumbo, he was regarded with terror in the slum district in which he lived. The other was Hank Borg, a sniffer, white, thin, not more than twenty years of age, his pinched rat-like face pitted with acne. He held a .38 automatic in his hand and his snake's eye glistened with an insane fever.

Henry felt a cold wave of fear like icy water run over him. The size of this gigantic Negro horrified him.

With one swift movement, Johnny grabbed the brief-case and stood up. Looking at him, Henry saw there was a thin circle of white around Johnny's mouth. Johnny backed away, watching Hank.

"Go ahead and shoot, creep," he said softly. "Abe will love it."

Hank said in a snarling whisper, "I'll bust your goddamn leg. Put that case back on the table."

Johnny continued to back away. He was now away from the desk and had space to manoeuvre.

"Take it easy, Colonel," he said. "The junkie daren't shoot. He's bluffing."

Hank looked uneasily at the Negro.

"Take him . . . we're wasting time."

The enormous Negro's brutal face split into a sneering grin.

"Come on, little man, hand it over."

Johnny dropped the brief-case on the floor beside him.

"Come and get it," he said, standing motionless, his hands hanging by his sides.

The Negro had to pass Henry and come around the desk to reach Johnny. He moved very swiftly. Henry, his old heart beating violently, slid out his long leg as the Negro swept past him. His Mexican booted foot caught the

Negro's ankle. The Negro stumbled, struggled to regain his balance as Johnny was on him, fingers laced, smashed down on the back of the Negro's neck, driving him to his knees. Johnny jumped back and kicked the Negro on the side of the face. The Negro's skin burst under the impact like an over-ripe tomato dropped on the floor and blood splashed on Johnny's shoe. The Negro grunted, shook his head and began to heave himself up, blood pouring down his face. Johnny waited until the dazed giant was on his knees, then he struck him a vicious karate blow on the side of his thick neck. The Negro's eyes rolled back and he flattened out on Abe's shabby carpet.

Johnny turned and looked at Hank who was backing away.

"Get out!" he said softly.

Hank turned and fled.

Johnny looked down at the bleeding Negro, then he looked at Henry.

"You all right?"

Henry was pressing his hand hard to his heart. He was breathing unevenly. These brief moments of violence had shaken him, but he nodded.

"Sure?"

"Yes ... I'm all right."

Johnny grinned.

"You've got guts, Colonel. I said it before and I'll say it again. That foot work of yours needed nerve. You handed this ape to me on a plate."

He caught hold of Jumbo's right ankle and dragged him out of the office, across the corridor to the top of the stairs. Then with a vicious kick, he propelled the great body down the long flight of stairs to land with a crash on the lower landing.

Abe, concealed by the bend of the corridor, watched this with his eyes bulging out of his head. When he was sure Johnny had returned to the office, he went up to Jumbo, slapped his face and dragged him upright.

Jumbo moaned, shaking his head.

"Get the hell out of here, you useless jerk!" Abe snarled, then he went to the elevator and took it to the ground floor, knowing now he just had to raise credit from somewhere.

Three hours and five minutes later, he returned to the office, an oily smile on his fat face. He placed a brief-case on the desk.

"All fixed, Johnny. It was tricky, but I got you your money," he said. "Go ahead and count it."

Johnny opened the brief-case, divided the money, giving Henry half. They counted it. The sum was for one hundred thousand dollars in $50 bills.

"Fine," Johnny said. He pushed two of the wash-leather bags over to Abe. Then he opened the third and took from it a treble rope of pearls. These he dropped into his pocket, then tossed the bag over to Abe.

"Hey! What do you think you are doing?" Abe exclaimed. "I've just bought those pearls!"

"No, you haven't. This is treachery money. I warned you not to play tricks," Johnny said. He walked over to Abe who cowered away from him. "The next time you pull a stunt like that on me, I'll break your neck." He moved to the door, nodding to Henry. "Let's go, Colonel."

Not looking at Abe, Henry followed him to the elevator.

In the meantime, Lisa and Harry had returned home. Although Lisa looked better for the sea trip, she was still in pain. The new drugs had done little for her. She was still short tempered and kept picking on Harry because he hadn't sold the Texan.

But by now, Harry was past caring about Lisa's criticisms. He had had three unforgettable days and two unforgettable nights with Tania, that alone was worth anything that Lisa threw at him.

He also knew that in two days' time there was to be the annual general meeting of the Cohen Self-Service Stores in San Francisco. Lisa always attended this meeting, and

Harry felt that he could duck out of it since he had been away from the office for so long. But it wasn't to be. Optimistically, he had already alerted Tania that he would be free for two nights so when Lisa announced that she didn't feel well enough to attend the meeting and that Harry must go as her representative, Harry nearly blew his stack. But he had no argument nor excuse to duck out, so he had to go.

That night, he sneaked out of the house and went with Tania to the apartment. He broke the news to her.

Tania nodded gravely.

"It is destiny, Harry. Do you believe in destiny?"

"Sure," Harry said. He wasn't interested in destiny right at this moment. "It's stinking bad luck. Anyway, there it is. I have to go."

"And she will be alone ... with her nurse?"

"And all the other servants ... you don't have to bother your head about her."

"She'll go to bed at ten-thirty as you told me she always does with a sleeping pill, I suppose?" Tania said, not looking at him. "It's sad for her, isn't it?"

"Oh, forget it." Harry put his arm around her. "Let me tell you something ... you are looking very over-dressed."

Tania smiled.

"That can be arranged very quickly ... she won't have friends while you are away?"

"No. When she entertains, I have to be there. Now come on, Tania! Get those clothes off!"

Harry returned around two o'clock in the morning to the house. He let himself in and moved silently to his room. Then he had a shock that sent a cold wave of blood rushing up his spine. At the far end of the corridor, he saw Lisa's bedroom door was open and the light was on.

"Harry?" The hard querulous voice struck terror in Harry's heart.

He braced himself and walked slowly down the corridor and paused in Lisa's doorway.

She was propped up in bed. A copy of *War and Peace* lay by her side. Her pinched, pain-ridden face was pale, her big eyes glittering.

"Where have you been?"

Harry realised unless he could bluff his way out of this situation, he was in serious trouble.

"Why, Lisa," he said, coming into the room and closing the door. "Why aren't you asleep? Are you in pain?"

"Where have you been?"

"I couldn't sleep. I went for a walk." He came to the bed and sat by her.

"A walk? At this time . . . it's after two. I don't believe you!"

"Lisa . . . please . . . " Harry forced a smile, aware sweat was running down his back. "You have enough problems of your own. I haven't told you . . . I sleep badly, I have things on my mind . . . I find when I can't sleep, the best thing to do is to get up, dress and take a walk . . . then when I come back I do sleep."

Her glittering eyes were suspicious.

"Have you found a whore?" she demanded and the viciousness in her voice chilled Harry's blood.

God! This is dangerous! he thought.

"Lisa . . . how could you say such a thing?" He had to convince her and although his hypocrisy sickened him, he continued, as he leaned forward, forcing his eyes to meet hers, "You and I are in this mess together. It is a mess . . . it's not what marriage should be, but because of you, I have accepted the situation. There is no other woman in my life except you. If you can't believe this, then I have failed you. I have told you before and I'm telling you again, that first time when you and I made love was the best ever. So wonderful, I can live with it now and for always."

Hearing himself say these words, Harry was ashamed of himself, but he was so frightened he let his lies flow.

She regarded him for a long, shattering moment, then she shrugged.

"All right, Harry, I understand. Get some sleep now. You have two busy days ahead of you."

Harry got slowly to his feet, scarcely believing she had accepted his story and wishing she didn't continue to stare at him so suspiciously.

"Yes ... I'm sure to sleep now."

As he reached the door, feeling he had saved the situation, she said, "Harry ... "

"Please don't go out walking again. It has upset me so. When I telephoned your room and got no answer, I was frightened. If you can't sleep, please come and talk to me. Will you?"

With a sinking heart, realising the trap he had walked into, Harry nodded.

"Of course, darling, I won't do it again."

Martha and Gilda were on the terrace when Henry came slowly across the blue and white tiles.

"Well, what happened?" Martha demanded. "Did you get the money?"

Henry sank into a chair. He was still feeling shaken.

"Gilda, my dear, would you get me a strong whisky?"

Seeing his grey, drawn face, Gilda went swiftly across the lounge to the bar.

"Did you get the money?" Martha banged her small, fat fist on the bamboo table.

"Johnny's got it."

"Johnny?" Martha's voice went up a note. "Where is he?"

"In his room."

"So Johnny's got it!" Martha shifted her bulk in the chair, making it creak. "So you can't handle him! It's a wonder I don't have a stroke!"

"Calm yourself. I would never have got it. At least, we have something," Henry said, hesitated, then went on, "Martha ... I've been thinking ... we're getting too old for this racket."

"You mean you're getting too old!" Martha snorted. "I'm not!"

Gilda came out, carrying a stiff whisky and soda.

"Thank you, my dear," Henry said, taking the glass from her. He swallowed half its contents, then set the glass down and touched his lips with his handkerchief.

"Stop acting like a goddamn ham!" Martha shouted. "What happened?"

Henry told her.

"The fact is, Martha, we wouldn't have got a dime if it hadn't been for Johnny. Abe was going to twist us. Those two thugs could have walked out with all the stuff and Abe would have sworn he knew nothing about them."

This news shook Martha. Her fat flesh quivered.

"I thought we could trust Abe."

"Can we trust anyone?"

Johnny came out on to the terrace. He tossed a bundle of $50 bills on the table.

"There you are ... sixty-six thousand, six hundred and sixty-seven bucks. Share it among yourselves. I've taken my share."

"How about that pearl necklace?" Martha snapped.

Johnny grinned at her.

"That's danger money ... I'm keeping it." He went over to a chair and sat down. "Now look ... what you three don't seem to realise is that you are in big time, but you are small timers. This is a rough, tough racket. It all falls on me, so I get the major share."

Martha began to explode, but a look from Henry stopped her.

Henry said quietly, "Yes, I follow your argument, Johnny, but let us be fair. This was Martha's brainwave. She has produced the brains and ... I admit it ... you the brawn. I think we should split the value of the pearls between us."

Johnny threw back his head and laughed.

"Who are you kidding? Who haggled with Abe? Who handled that black ape? Who got the jewels anyway?

Okay, it was her idea, but any dope can dream up an idea, but that doesn't mean he can carry it out. None of you could have swung this job and got a hundred grand out of Abe if I hadn't handled it ... so shut up!" He turned to look at Gilda. "Do you want to eat out? I need a change. There's a sea food restaurant I fancy ... want to come along?"

Gilda stared with startled surprise, but she got quickly to her feet.

"Yes ... I would like that."

"Okay. Throw some clothes on and we'll go."

Her face slightly flushed, Gilda hurried away to her room.

He's nibbling at the bait, she thought happily as she slipped out of her bikini. Play it cool, baby, and you'll land him.

On the terrace, Johnny lit a cigarette.

"The day after tomorrow," he said, "I'll take a look at the Crails' house. I guess I can get in if I wear that electrician's uniform. Nothing like a uniform to fool the suspicious. Then we'll do the job. It's worth six hundred and fifty grand. I'll sell the stuff to Bernie Baum. I've had enough of Abe. Bernie can have it for three hundred. He'll jump at it for that price. That's two hundred grand for you three."

"Who the hell do you think you are?" Martha screamed furiously. "I make the plans! Henry fixes the prices!"

"Oh, shut up, Fatso," Johnny said. "I'm handling this. Neither of you have a hope of dealing with Baum. You're too old!"

Seeing Martha was about to explode, Henry said quietly, "He's right, Martha. Okay, Johnny, we leave it to you."

Martha was so angry she couldn't trust herself to speak. She sat there, her fat flesh quivering.

Gilda came out on to the terrace. She was wearing a simple blue frock. She looked cool and lovely. Johnny regarded her and Gilda thought there could be sudden interest in his eyes.

They went off together in the Cadillac.

"Got your money yet?" Johnny asked as he sent the big car fast along the beach road.

"Henry's keeping it for me."

"That wise?"

"I trust Henry."

"Good for you."

There was a long pause, then Gilda said, "You should watch out for Martha. She hates you."

Johnny laughed.

"That fat old slug? What can she do to me?"

"Don't be too sure ... she's dangerous."

Johnny laughed again.

The restaurant Johnny took her to had a jetty out in the sea, and on this jetty, the tables were set. There were coloured lights, a band playing soft swing and the place was crowded.

As Gilda walked to their table, she saw the male diners were looking at her with alert interest. She tilted her chin and swung her hips a little. It pleased her to be looked at and so obviously admired.

The service was quick and smooth and the food excellent. While they were eating lobster cocktails, Gilda became aware of a woman diner alone on the other side of the aisle who continually stared at Johnny. This woman was around thirty-six or possibly thirty-eight: slim, blonde, wearing an expensive but plain white dress. She had classical features, cold, hard and sensual. Her steel blue eyes scarcely left Johnny.

Johnny seemed relaxed and unaware that he was being scrutinised.

"We do the final job the night after next," he said as he finished the cocktail. "Hmmm ... that was good."

"It was marvellous. The Crails' place?"

"That's it. Then I'm off."

Gilda felt a little pang run through her.

"You mean you're leaving?"

He looked up, frowning.

"Of course. You can't imagine I'm staying in this plush dump longer than I can help, do you?"

Gilda pressed her hands to her breasts.

"Where are you going?"

"Oh, for God's sake! I told you ... Carmel."

The sole in lobster sauce with truffles was placed before them. Gilda found she had lost her appetite.

"Johnny ... "

He was eating. He glanced up.

"Huh?"

"Must you rush off? We have the villa for another two weeks. Won't you stay until then?" Gilda moved the food on her plate with her fork. "We could get to know each other better."

Johnny grinned. He forked a piece of lobster meat to his mouth.

"There's no reason why we shouldn't get to know each other better after dinner, is there?"

Gilda stiffened, feeling blood rush to her face. She stared at him.

Johnny regarded her, saw her shocked expression, grimaced, then shrugged.

"Okay, let's skip it."

They ate in silence. Gilda felt the food would choke her. Then the woman's stare finally attracted Johnny's attention. He had been vaguely aware of being watched and now the feeling had become acute. He turned his head slowly and looked at the woman who stared directly at him as she toyed with her wine glass. The brash, sensual look told him here was a blatant invitation. For two or three seconds they continued to stare at each other, then Gilda, watching, said sharply, "Are you dreaming or something, Johnny?"

Johnny dragged his eyes from the woman.

"A real pair of hot pants over on my right," he said, grinning. "Is she after a man!"

"Yes. A horrible woman!" Gilda said, trying to keep the alarm out of her voice. "A whore!"

Johnny smiled cynically.

"Do you think so? I don't. She's honest. She's telling me that she wants me. I dig for a woman like that. She saves a man time. This no-I-don't-yes-I-might drag bores me."

Gilda pushed her plate aside. She felt slightly sick.

"I see. I'm sorry I'm boring you."

Johnny shrugged indifferently.

"Well, if that's the way you are made, that's the way you're made ... simple as that."

The night, the moon, the sea, the coloured lights, the music all collapsed on Gilda.

"Is it?" Her voice trembled. "Isn't there such a thing as love?"

Johnny leaned back in his chair, his eyebrows lifting.

"Oh, come on, baby, grow up! What is love but sex?" He leaned forward, staring at her, his eyes hot and intent. "Let's get the hell out of here. Let's go down to the beach. I have a yen for you and I know you have a yen for me. I can see it ... it's there in your eyes. Let's get laid tonight. Come on, baby, let's set the night on fire."

Gilda's hands gripped her bag, her nails digging into the soft fabric.

"How can you talk to me this way? Johnny! I love you!" Her lips trembled and her face was pale.

An expression of disgust and suspicion crossed Johnny's face.

"Oh, God! One of those! Listen, baby, I ... "

Gilda got to her feet.

Speaking softly so no one except Johnny could hear, she said, her voice unsteady, "Enjoy yourself. Take that whore. You can walk home. Martha was right ... you are no good," and she moved swiftly from the table and away down the aisle.

Johnny remained motionless. A sudden black rage surged through him. He had to make an effort to restrain himself from sweeping the contents of the table on to the floor.

Love ... marriage ... he didn't want that! A woman could have no permanent place in his life. He wanted his garage, his fast cars and around him, men who knew and talked cars.

Always goddamn complications, he thought savagely. The moment he had seen Gilda he had wanted her physically, but not permanently. He knew he wouldn't want her when she had to dye her greying hair. He wanted her now! The thought of living permanently with her when the sex thing had gone cold and she ran his home, grumbling about how he dirtied things up, providing him with the deadly, dreary meals for lunch and dinner and dinner and lunch, day after day, nagging him if he were late when he was working on some car ... hell! No! That he couldn't take!

A low, musical voice said, "Did she walk out on you?"

Johnny stiffened and found the blonde woman had crossed the aisle and was now sitting where Gilda had been sitting.

Looking at her, seeing her heavy breasts under the white frock and the cold, sophisticated beauty, Johnny felt a surge of lust run through him.

"That's what she did," he said. "She's the virgin type."

The woman laughed. Her laugh was attractive. She threw her head back, revealing a beautiful throat: her teeth were perfect.

"I thought so. But I'm not. What's your name?"

"Johnny."

"Johnny ... I like that. I'm Helene." The steel blue eyes hotly devoured him. "Why waste time, Johnny? I know what you want. I want what you want. Shall we go?"

Johnny snapped his fingers at a passing waiter for his check.

"Oh, forget it," she said impatiently, getting to her feet. "They know me here. The check will be taken care of."

So what? Johnny thought. I'll give this bitch value for money.

With the eyes of everyone in the restaurant on him, he followed the woman down the jetty.

Martha had just finished dinner when Gilda came up the terrace steps. Henry, who was pouring himself a brandy, looked up, surprised.

"Where's Johnny?" Martha demanded, seeing Gilda was alone.

Her eyes bright with tears, Gilda didn't pause. She threw over her shoulder, "I don't know, and who the hell cares?"

Her bedroom door slammed.

Martha was about to select a coffee cream from a large box of chocolates Henry had brought her. She paused and stared at Henry.

"Now, what's going on?"

Henry shook his head: his expression a little sad.

"Young people . . . it's the salt in their lives to quarrel. Don't you remember when you were young?"

Martha snorted.

"He's no good. I knew it the moment I saw him. He's a goddamn sonofabitch!"

"I wouldn't go as far as saying that," Henry said and sipped his brandy. "He's made us a lot of money."

While Gilda was lying face down on her bed, crying, Johnny was sitting beside the blonde woman as she drove her Mercury Cougar along the beach road. From time to time, she put her hand high up on his thigh, squeezing his muscles.

"You're not just all muscle, are you, Johnny?" she asked.

Johnny laughed.

"Wait and see."

121

She glanced at him, her eyes alight, her lips curved in a sensuous smile.

"*You* won't be disappointed. I'm just wondering if I will be."

"Wait and see. Where are we going?"

"To my place. My dear, aged, impotent husband is in New York." Her fingers dug deeply into Johnny's muscles. Impatiently, he swept her hand away.

They eventually drove through a high, open gateway and pulled up outside an imposing-looking house that was in darkness.

"The slaves are asleep," Helene said as they got out of the car. "Don't make a noise."

A few seconds later, they were in a big, luxuriously furnished bedroom. Helene walked to the bed, then turned and faced Johnny as he came towards her. She was breathing rapidly and there was a queer, almost insane look in her steel blue eyes. She swung her evening bag and hit Johnny violently across his face. The metal clasp of the bag cut the side of his nose. He started back, staring at her in angry astonishment as he felt blood running down his face and on to his shirt, then as she swung the bag again, he caught her wrist and wrenched the bag out of her hand.

With blood dripping over both of them, Johnny tore the dress off her and flung her on the bed.

Around four o'clock the following morning, Martha woke, feeling hungry. She lay in the dark, trying to make up her mind whether to try to sleep or whether to get up and visit the refrigerator. As always, the refrigerator won. She turned on the light, put on a wrap and plodded to the kitchen. There was a mess of cold spaghetti, onions and tomatoes with some minced veal that took her fancy. She was reaching for the bowl when she heard a door open and then shut softly. Frowning, she went into the corridor. Johnny was moving silently to his bedroom. Seeing her, outlined in the kitchen door, he paused.

"Hello," he said. "Are you stuffing your gut?"

"Never mind what I'm doing!" Martha snapped. "What are you doing?"

"What do you think? I'm going to bed."

Martha turned on the corridor light. She stared at Johnny, a cold wash of fear running over her.

Dried blood caked his face. He had a cut on the side of his nose. There were big splashes of blood on his white shirt.

"What have you been doing?" Martha demanded, her voice quavering.

"Making love to a buzz saw," Johnny said and grinned. "Good night," and he went into his bedroom and closed the door.

Martha found she had lost her appetite. Turning off the lights, she returned to her bed. *Making love to a buzz saw.* What did that mean? She had a cold presentiment that Johnny was edging them all into the worst kind of trouble. All that blood! What had he been doing?

While this was going on, Harry Lewis lay sleepless in a bedroom at the San Francisco Hilton Hotel. The annual general meeting had gone off slickly and with no trouble. All the stockholders were happy, but Harry wasn't. He had been acutely aware that the directors of Cohen's Self-Service Stores regarded him as a gigolo. The Trustees of the estate scarcely bothered to speak to him. Although he had made notes, asked questions, collected all the papers relating to the meeting for Lisa, he knew these hatchet-faced men regarded him as a poor joke.

The bastards! Harry thought, tossing in his bed. My God! One of these days, if I get the chance, I'll pay them back!

Then to try to quieten his seething mind, he turned his thoughts to Tania. He thought of her with affection. But what was he to do about seeing her in the future? He dared not sneak out of his room at night again. This would be taking too great a risk. He realised the trap he was in. Sunday morning would be his only chance now, and Lisa might even stop that. Still worrying, still trying to find a solution, he eventually fell asleep.

It was a little after eight o'clock the following morning, when he was awakened by the telephone bell buzzing discreetly. Yawning, he answered.

"Yes?"

"Mr Lewis? This is Dr Gourley calling from Paradise City."

Harry came awake with a jerk. He sat up.

"Yes? What is it?"

He listened to the calm, quiet voice and cold sweat broke out on his face and body.

"What are you saying?" His voice shot up. "Lisa dead! Murdered! You're crazy? What are you saying?"

He threw off the sheet and sat now on the edge of the bed.

The quiet, calm voice continued to speak.

Harry shut his eyes. He couldn't believe what the doctor was telling him.

"Yes, of course I'll come. Yes ... the first available plane. The ... what was that?"

"The Esmaldi necklace has been stolen," Gourley said. "This seems to be the motive for the murder, Mr Lewis. The police are here. They naturally want to talk to you."

Harry hung up. He remained motionless.

Lisa dead! Murdered!

He thought of her ... what she had done for him ... her tempers ... her poor pain-ridden scraggy body ... her pitiful hooked nose.

Murdered!

He drew in a long, shuddering breath.

He continued to sit on the edge of the bed, trying to control his emotions.

Lisa dead! It didn't seem possible. Then it slowly dawned on him that now he was free. Now he owned everything that she had owned. Now he had no need to plot and plan nor to tell lies ...

He got unsteadily to his feet and began to pack.

Flo wheeled the breakfast trolley into Martha's room. She smiled happily, showing her enormous white teeth.

"I have a little change for you, Miss Martha."

Martha sat up in bed, leaned forward to peer as Flo removed the silver cover. The six lightly poached eggs, lying on beds of *foie gras* on thin toast and four slices of smoked salmon done in rolls made Martha's eyes widen with pleasure.

"That looks like a masterpiece, Flo," she said. "A very happy idea."

Flo beamed. She was always thinking up changes for Martha's breakfast and she could see the fat woman was delighted.

Martha began to eat, then seeing it was approaching nine o'clock, she turned on her transistor radio, permanently tuned to the Paradise City radio station. Martha believed in listening in to all the local news.

She had finished one egg and was starting on the second when the time signal for nine o'clock pipped.

Three minutes later, her meal forgotten, she was out of bed, her fat face like cold pork fat, sweat beads on her forehead. She struggled into her wrap as she lumbered down the corridor and out on to the terrace.

Henry and Gilda were drinking coffee in the sunshine. The sight of Martha looking wild and terrified, brought both of them to their feet.

It took Martha several seconds to become coherent. Then she told them what the radio announcer had been broadcasting. Lisa Lewis, the richest woman in Paradise City and possibly the fourth richest woman in the world, had been battered to death and the famous Esmaldi necklace had been stolen.

"It's that bastard! ... That sonofabitch, Johnny!" Martha wailed. "He knew she had the necklace! He wanted to steal it! I told him no! But he's done it and the bitch-bastard has killed her! I caught him coming in last night ... covered in blood! God! We're fixed, Henry. That goddamn necklace is insured by Maddox. Do you hear? We're fixed!" she dropped into a chair, moaning.

Henry suddenly felt very old and feeble. His heart began to beat sluggishly. He couldn't think.

"I – I don't believe it," he muttered. "Johnny wouldn't do a thing like that."

"I tell you I saw him come sneaking in last night! It was four o'clock. He was smothered in blood!" Martha screamed, thumping her enormous bosom, trying to catch her breath. "Who else could have opened a Raysons' safe? He knew the blueprint! The bastard intended to gyp us! He went there, she caught him, so he killed her. Then he took the necklace! Henry! We're fixed!"

"Shut up!" Gilda exclaimed, her voice hard and shrill. "How do you know he did it?"

She rushed across the terrace and down the corridor to Johnny's room. She threw open the door, then she paused, her hand flying to her mouth.

Johnny was sleeping. A deep cut of dried blood showed on his nose. A bloodstained shirt lay on the floor. There were scratches on his naked arms ... nail scratches.

Gilda felt a cold shudder run through her. She went over to him, grabbed his shoulder and shook him awake.

CHAPTER SIX

When Harry returned to Paradise City, he found the Rolls waiting at the airport with To-To at the wheel. To-To seemed stunned. When Harry questioned him about Lisa, the Jap just shook his head, muttering, "Bad ... bad ... bad," and that's all Harry could get out of him.

The Rolls pulled up outside the house and Harry ran up the steps. He saw there were five police cars parked in the drive and when he walked into the hall, the place seemed full of plain-clothes and uniformed officers.

Police Captain Fred Terrell came out of the living-room and introduced himself. This wasn't necessary. Harry had often seen Terrell on the golf course and knew him to be a sound, efficient police chief.

As Terrell walked with Harry into the living-room, he said, "The robbery and the murder took place between eleven o'clock and three o'clock. That's the nearest the M.O. can place it."

Harry sat down. He was still in a state of shock. As he lit a cigarette, his hands trembled.

"How did it happen?"

"It's a bit of a mystery." Terrell lowered his bulk into an armchair. "Right now, Mr Lewis, we're wondering if it could be an inside job."

Harry stiffened and stared at him.

"What the hell do you mean?"

"Your staff are top suspects for the moment," Terrell said quietly. "We've checked all the doors. The locks on the front door, the side door and the patio door are special and they haven't been tampered with. A window in your study was found open. This seems to have been opened to make us think the killer got in that way, but we're satisfied the window was opened from the inside."

"But none of the staff ... "

"Just a moment. How long have you had the nurse ... Helgar?"

"This is ridiculous! Helgar was devoted to my wife!"

"How long has she been here?"

"Ever since my wife had her accident ... two years."

"Here's another little problem, Mr Lewis. The Raysons' safe is burglar-proof. I know these safes well. Who else beside you knew how to open it and turn off the alarm?"

"My wife, of course ... and ... Helgar."

"The Jap or the other staff?"

"No."

Terrell nodded.

"The safe was found open when Helgar discovered the murder. You see what I'm getting at? This is a very complicated safe. Whoever opened it must have known where the hidden switches are located. We've already checked on this with Hacket, the local agent. Unless you know better, Mr Lewis, the only people who could have opened the safe are Hacket, the fitter, yourself and Helgar. We are now checking on Hacket and the fitter. We know them. They are first-class people, and I'm sure we can rule them out." Terrell pulled at his moustache. "So that leaves you and Helgar ... you were in 'Frisco, so that leaves Helgar."

"It's wrong. Helgar wouldn't have done it," Harry said. "She was devoted to Lisa."

Terrell lifted his heavy shoulders.

"From what I hear the Esmaldi necklace would be a big temptation."

Harry got to his feet.

"Well, I have to leave all this to you, Captain. Now, I would like to see my wife."

Terrell looked at him, then shook his head.

"I would advise against that, Mr Lewis. I know how you are feeling, but you should avoid that experience. Helgar has identified her. You see, this is a shocking thing . . . the murder was brutal and savage. The killer struck your wife with a small bronze statue that I understand stood in the hall. There were repeated blows. The killer meant to kill her. She is not a sight you should see."

Harry turned pale.

"I see." He felt as if he were going to be sick. "You'll excuse me. If you want me, I'll be in my study," and he went slowly and unsteadily from the room.

As he left, Fred Hess, head of the Homicide Squad, a short, fat man with cold, shrewd eyes, came in.

"Nothing, Chief," he said in disgust. 'No fingerprints . . . no clues. Doc Gourley says the killer will have bloodstains on him. I've been over Helgar's room . . . nothing. We've checked the rooms of the rest of the staff . . . nothing. All the same, I'm willing to bet this is an inside job. The open window points to it. It was definitely opened from the inside."

"Unless it was done deliberately to make us think it was an inside job," Terrell said thoughtfully.

Hess scratched his head.

"Yeah. Then how did the killer get in? Whoever it was knew how to open the safe. I've been wondering about Lewis."

"He was in 'Frisco. He has a cast-iron alibi."

"Sure, but he benefits . . . now, he's worth millions. Maybe he hired someone to do the job. He could have given the killer the front door key and told him how to open the safe."

Terrell brooded over this, then he nodded.

"You have an idea there, Fred. Yes . . . if Helgar didn't do it, then Lewis is our top suspect. Suppose we start digging into his background?"

Mrs Lowenstein, grimacing, sipped her hot lemon juice and water. In another two weeks she would be leaving the

Clinic, satisfied that she had shed at least two stone of unwanted fat. She turned on the radio to listen to the nine o'clock news. She was so shocked when she heard that Lisa Lewis had been murdered, that the foolproof Raysons' safe had been opened and the famous Esmaldi necklace had been stolen that for some minutes she lay in her bed, unable to think and having difficulty with her breathing.

She had never liked Lisa, but this was a terrible thing and she wondered if she should telephone Harry (who she also disliked) and offer condolences. She decided against this. How could anyone break into a Raysons' safe? She felt a rush of blood to her head. If Lisa's safe had been broken into, so could hers!

She snatched up the telephone receiver and called her residence. After a little delay, Baines, her butler, answered.

"Baines? Have you heard about Mrs Lewis? Is my jewellery safe?"

Having finished a somewhat heavy breakfast, Baines found this question absurd and irritating.

"Of course it is, madam. Your jewels are in the safe."

"I know that! So was Mrs Lewis's necklace, but it has gone! Baines, go to the safe and see! Have you been to the safe since I have been here?"

"Certainly not, madam."

"Then go and see immediately. I will hold on."

"Very well, madam." Baines managed to convey in his disapproving tone that madam was an hysterical, old fool.

Four minutes later, just when Mrs Lowenstein was beginning to boil over with impatience, Baines came back on the line. His voice sounded unsteady and shocked.

"I regret to tell you, madam, the jewels are missing," he said.

"All of them?" Mrs Lowenstein screeched.

"I'm afraid so, madam."

"Call the police! I'm coming at once!"

While this was going on, Mrs Alec Jackson, who was once a famous Danish model and who still kept her figure although now fifty-two years of age, picked up the nine o'clock news while sitting on the deck of her husband's yacht, anchored in the Miami harbour.

"Alec! Did you hear?" she demanded, turning off the transistor.

Her husband, stout, sixty years of age who drank whisky for breakfast, dragged his eyes from the financial column of the *Miami Times* and scowled at her.

"Heard ... what?"

"Don't you ever listen to anything? Lisa Lewis has been murdered and her necklace has been stolen!"

Jackson laid down his newspaper and whistled.

"Murdered? Well! A bit of luck for Harry. He'll come into all her money."

"Alec!" Mona Jackson was outraged. "Can't you think of anything but money? You should be ashamed of yourself!"

Jackson shrugged.

"Don't get so worked up ... it's not good for you."

"The thieves broke into her safe. The safe's the same as mine. If they can do that, they could have also stolen my jewellery!"

"Oh, for God's sake! Your trinkets are perfectly safe." Jackson reached for his glass. "Well, fancy Harry coming into all that money. Boy! He'll be worth millions. I bet he'll have himself a ball."

"How can you be so callous? Lisa! Murdered!"

"Oh, come off it, Mona. You know you hated her! Only the other night you said she was a two-faced bitch."

"Alec! Will you stop being disgusting? I want you to telephone David Hacket immediately and ask him to check my safe to see if my jewellery is still there."

Jackson gaped at her.

"Of course it's still there!"

"Will you telephone David Hacket or do I have to?"

Knowing from the expression on her face that there

would be no peace for him if he didn't telephone, Jackson groaned and heaved himself to his feet.

"Women!" he exclaimed bitterly. "David will think I'm crazy."

"I don't give a damn what he thinks! Tell him to go to the house and open the safe and call back."

Jackson walked across the quay to the nearest telephone booth. After a little delay, he got through to David Hacket, the sales manager of Raysons' safes. The two men played golf together most week-ends and they were good friends.

"David . . . this is Alec," Jackson said. "Sorry to bother you with this, but Mona's heard about Lisa Lewis's robbery. She wants you to go to our place and check the safe to see if her goddamn jewels are okay. Do you mind?"

There was a long pause, then Hacket said, "No, of course not. I'll go right away. I – I hope they are safe."

Jackson stiffened.

"What do you mean . . . hope they are safe?"

"You'll read about it tomorrow, so you may as well know now. Another of our safes has been broken into. God knows how it was done. Mrs Lowenstein has lost everything."

"Good grief! If I tell Mona she'll blow her stack. Look, David, will you get out there right away. Call me back as soon as you can. I'll wait." He gave the call booth's number. "If Mona has lost her stuff . . . I don't know how I'll live with her!"

"I'll call you back as soon as I can."

Jackson ordered a double whisky and soda and sat down to wait. An hour and a half later, Hacket called back.

"I'm sorry to tell you, Alec," he said in a strained voice, "but you've been robbed . . . everything in the safe has gone."

Johnny came out on to the terrace. He had thrown on a pair of slacks and a long-sleeved sweat shirt to hide the scratches on his arms. His hair was tousled and he needed a shave: he looked what he felt – a wreck.

At the sight of him, Martha cowered back in her chair.

"Keep away from me, you murderer!" she shrilled.

"Oh, shut up!" Johnny snarled. His eyes were uneasy and a nerve twitched by his mouth. "I didn't do it! Get that into your thick skull. Do you hear me? I didn't do it!"

"You're a liar!" Martha screamed. "You went after that necklace. You were planning to gyp us! She caught you opening the safe and you killed her, you vicious, murdering sonofabitch!"

Henry said sharply, "Martha, please! Let me talk to Johnny."

"Talk to him! He's fixed us! Murderer! I wish I had never set eyes on him!" Martha hid her face in her fat hands and began to moan.

Johnny came over to where Henry was sitting and stood over him.

"I didn't do it," he repeated, his voice unsteady. "I was with a woman all night. Ask Gilda ... she knows. There was this woman after me. Gilda and I fell out. She left. This woman took me to her home."

Henry looked at Gilda who was standing, white-faced, behind Johnny. She nodded.

"Who was this woman?" Henry asked.

"Her name's Helene Booth ... she's a rich nympho. Her husband is in New York on a trip. She picked on me. I didn't leave her place until close on four this morning," Johnny said. "She was crazy. She hit me and scratched me up. That blood Martha saw was my blood!"

"He's lying!" Martha screamed. "I don't believe a word of what he says! He stole the necklace and killed that woman!"

Dabbing his sweating face with his silk handkerchief, Henry regarded Johnny.

"Is that the story you are going to tell the police if they catch up with you, Johnny?"

133

"Why not . . . it's the truth!"

"Do you imagine a wealthy, married woman would support such a tale? Do you imagine she would admit sleeping with you?"

Johnny sat down. His legs seemed to collapse under him.

"I swear it's the truth!"

"I believe you," Gilda said, coming over to him and putting her hand on his shoulder. "I do believe you, Johnny."

"You would, you besotted, stupid little fool!" Martha raged. "I warned you! He's no good! He's vicious! Now, he's fixed us!"

"If you don't shut your fat mouth, I'll shut it for you!" Johnny shouted furiously.

"Yes! That's right!" Martha yelled back. "Go ahead and kill me as you killed that woman!"

"Stop it!" Henry exclaimed. "Now, listen to me . . . we're in one hell of a mess. I believe Johnny . . . I don't think he killed this woman, but that doesn't help us. There's only one thing to do . . . we must get out of here fast! We have the money. We'll split up. We'll get out right away."

Johnny regarded the old man's white, frightened face, then he shook his head.

"No, that's panic tactics," he said steadily. "We have rented this villa for two more weeks. The rent's paid. If we bolt now we put the searchlight of suspicion slap on us. That's not the way to handle it. We've got to use our heads. I didn't kill that woman, but someone did. Someone who knew how to open that very secret safe. What we've got to do is find the killer." He paused, then went on, "If the cops catch me, I go down for murder, but you three will go down with me. We're all in this together whether you like it or not. So we stick right here." He raised his hand as Martha began to say something. "You shut up! What you have to remember is that even if they suspect we have done this job, they can't prove it! Before they can even arrest us, they have to have some kind of proof and we know we have left no clues nor fingerprints. We have to keep our nerve. We run now and they'll come after us. We stick here for the next two weeks, taking it easy, living like people on a vacation, and we have a ninety-nine per cent chance of them never even investigating us. But there is one thing we have to do: we have to get our money out of here. If the cops search the place and find all that money, we are cooked!"

"I'm getting out!" Martha said violently. "I'm taking my money and I'm going!"

"You're not!" Johnny shouted at her. "You're putting your money in a safe deposit box and you're staying right here."

"Yes," Henry said. "We run now, Martha, and we are really fixed. I can see that now. Our one hope is to bluff it out. Johnny's right."

Martha began to cry.

"This sonofabitch spoilt the nicest breakfast I've had in months," she snivelled.

Johnny turned impatiently away from her.

"As soon as the bank opens, I'll go down with the money."

"You're not touching *my* share!" Martha shrilled. "Do you think ... "

"Oh, shut up!" Johnny half-started to his feet, then restrained himself. He turned to Henry. "You know what I think? I think that woman's husband did it. Look what he stands to gain ... all her money ... millions. Who else beside us knew how to open the safe?"

"That doesn't help us," Henry pointed out.

"It could. I'm going to have this guy watched. It's worth spending money on. I'm going to stick a team of private eyes on him. We can't handle it ... it's a professional job."

"Listen!" Gilda said sharply.

They heard the sound of an approaching car coming up the avenue, travelling at speed.

Johnny's face tightened. He got to his feet.

"They couldn't have got on to us this fast!" He walked quickly to the side of the terrace to peer over the balcony, looking down at the drive-in to the villa. He felt his heart skip a beat as a big black car swept through the open gateway and squealed to a stop outside the front door where he lost sight of it.

He turned, his face pale under his tan.

"Could be the cops," he said. "If they find the money ..."

They heard the front door bell ring. They heard Flo open the door and then heard her catch her breath in a surprised cry. As Johnny started across the terrace, Abe Schulman, followed by the gigantic Jumbo, came out on to the terrace.

The unexpected sight of Abe startled the four. Abe's face was shining with sweat and the colour of old tallow. He came across the terrace and dropped a brief-case on the table.

"There's your stuff!" he said, his voice high pitched. "I want my money back! Come on ... a hundred thousand! I want it now!"

There was a long pause. Henry and Martha looked at each other. Neither of them knew what to say, then Johnny came forward, his face hard, his eyes glittering.

"Are you crazy, Abe?" he said. "What money? What do you mean ... our stuff?"

"Don't give me that! I caught the six o'clock news. This is murder! I don't go along with murder! The deal's off! Give me my money back!"

"Deal? Money? What the hell are you talking about? We haven't done a deal with you, Abe," Johnny said quietly. "And what's all this about murder?"

"This is something you don't talk yourself out of," Abe snarled. "This stuff ... " he slapped the brief-case, "is red hot. No one will touch it and I'm not touching it! I want my money back!"

"What money? I don't understand."

Abe stared evilly at Johnny.

"Do you think you can bluff me, you small time creep?" he snarled. "I was in this racket before you were even a thought in your father's mind! That's one thing you don't do! There's the stuff! I don't give a goddamn what you do with it! I do know you're giving me my money back!"

Johnny reached for a cigarette from a box on the table. He lit it. Watching, Gilda saw that his hands were steady.

"Sorry, Abe . . . no deal. You bought the stuff . . . you're stuck with it. Run away," Johnny said.

"Is that your last word . . . it isn't mine," Abe said. "Are you going to be that stupid?"

"I said run away and take your black ape with you."

"Okay, so now I'll tell you something," Abe said. "I'm leaving this stuff with you. I'm not going to get caught with it. This stuff is sheer dynamite. One thing I'll never get hooked with is a murder rap. It's so important to me not to get hooked with a murder rap, I'm ready to kiss one hundred thousand grand good-bye. But, my young, slick bluffer, I'll tell you what I am going to do. When I leave here, I'm going to call the cops . . . an anonymous tip-off. I'll tell them who stole the Esmaldi necklace and murdered Lisa Lewis. I'll tell them who stole the Lowensteins' and the Jacksons' collections. Then when you have a swarm of tough cops in your lap, don't kid yourself you can drag me into it. I haven't got the stuff. You have. You can't prove I've ever had it. Maybe you imagine you can bluff eight or nine tough bulls who'll question you for hours and probably knock your slick teeth out of your slick mouth. If you think you can, so okay, then you stick to my money, but if you don't think you can, give me my money!"

"The cops have nothing on us," Johnny said. "You don't bluff me, Abe. Beat it!"

"They have nothing on you?" Abe said and showed his small, yellow teeth. "I'll tell you what they will have on you: they'll find out you once worked for Raysons' safes. They'll find out you have a record for violence and a

137

prison record. They'll find out Martha has served five years for jewel robbery. They'll find out Henry has been in a cell for fifteen years. Can you imagine that fat old woman standing up under hours of tough cop interrogation? Can you imagine the Colonel standing up to the same treatment? Can you imagine yourself – tough as you think you are – taking a police beating while they question you? I'm not bluffing, my young creep. I want my money back or I make a phone call."

Johnny's eyes turned vicious.

"I could kill you, Abe, and your black ape, couldn't I?"

"Go ahead and try," Abe said, grinning. "See where it gets you. Where's my money?"

Johnny stubbed out his cigarette. He hesitated for a long moment, then looking at Henry, he shrugged.

"So the Jew gets his money," he said.

Around midday, as the last of the plain-clothes officers were leaving the Lewis's residence, a sleek Cadillac pulled up outside the front entrance and Warren Weidman, Lisa's attorney, got out. He walked past the last of the detectives as they came down the steps without looking at them. Warren Weidman regarded policemen as servants of the public: men who served a purpose, but who were of no consequence. Police Chief Terrell, with whom he was on speaking terms, had long gone.

Warren Weidman was a tall, heavily-built man with a whisky complexion and all the signs of liking luxury living. Immaculately dressed in a dark suit, he was wearing a black tie which his secretary had provided to replace the silver grey tie with a small horse's head in red in the centre. When Weidman was not at his desk, he was usually to be found either in some plush restaurant or on the racecourse.

To-To, who knew him well, led him silently to Harry's study, knocked and opened the door.

Weidman entered to find Harry sitting slumped in an armchair, smoking, a glass of whisky at his elbow.

Since the news had broken, the telephone had rung ceaselessly. All Lisa's so-called friends were offering condolences. Harry's own personal friends, now they realised he would be one of the richest men in the world, also rang him. Finally, Harry could stand it no longer and had told the telephone operator to route all calls to his office. He doubted if Miss Bernstein could cope with the sudden telephone traffic, but he didn't care. When he told her what to expect, she sounded hysterical, and he decided the first thing he would do when the dust settled would be to get rid of her. This gave him slight satisfaction, but he was still in shock and felt wretched.

He couldn't believe that Lisa was up there in her bedroom, dead and battered into something Terrell had said he shouldn't see. He had never loved Lisa, but he had pitied her. What a death! he kept thinking. For some vicious thug to have crept into her room and smashed a bronze statue down on her face while she was sleeping, defenceless, and to have kept on hitting that poor, pain-ridden unattractive face until she was dead. The thought turned Harry's stomach.

He had been sitting in the chair now for three hours, listening to the tramp of feet overhead and down the stairs and along the corridors of his home, to the sound of hushed men's voices who didn't give a damn about Lisa but who only thought of the killer.

A savage and brutal murder, Terrell had said. If an experienced police officer talked like that, Harry cringed to think what had happened to her.

When he heard a tap on the door and the door swung open, he stiffened and sat upright.

Weidman came quietly into the room.

"My dear fellow," he said in his melodious tones, coming over to Harry. "I can't tell you ... shocking ... I came as quickly as I could. I am entirely at your service."

He put down a bulky brief-case and sat in a chair opposite Harry. "Is there anything you want me to do?"

Harry had never liked Weidman although he knew him to be a shrewd and brilliant attorney. He shook his head.

"No, nothing right now. I – I ... well, I'm trying to adjust myself. Could we meet later? I'm in a complete mental mess right now."

"Of course." Weidman shifted his large body more firmly into the armchair. "I understand completely, but there are one or two things of importance we will have to attend to." He gave his quick, sympathetic, professional smile. "There's the Esmaldi necklace. I must put in an immediate claim. It's worth three hundred and fifty thousand and it is fully insured. As you know it has been willed to the Fine Arts Museum, Washington. There is a little problem there to sort out. We must put in a claim at once. May I go ahead?"

"Do whatever you like," Harry said indifferently. He wanted this well-fed looking man to leave him alone.

"Then there's the funeral. Mrs Lewis desired to be cremated. I will attend to all the details if you wish me to do so."

"Yes."

"Then there's the will, Mr Lewis."

Harry felt he couldn't bear any more of this. He waved his hand impatiently.

"We can go into all that later, can't we?"

"Of course, but I think you might want to know, Mr Lewis, that everything comes to you ... everything. The chain of stores, the house, all the estate, the stocks and bonds, the yacht ... everything. Mrs Lewis has left it to you to make bequests to anyone you think deserves them ... Miss Helgar, To-To, the rest of the staff and anyone else you might have in mind."

Harry stared at Weidman.

"Everything to me?" he repeated, and he felt a wave of

emotion run through him so that he had to fight against tears.

So Lisa in spite of her bitchy ways, in spite of her temper, in spite of her jealousy, must have loved him. She wouldn't have left everything to him like that unless she had really loved him.

"Yes." Seeing Harry's distress, Weidman got to his feet. "We can go over all this later, Mr Lewis. I'll leave you now. I understand your feelings. Please accept my deepest sympathy." He started for the door, then paused, "Oh, there is one little thing I should mention."

Harry nearly screamed to him to get out, but he controlled himself.

"What is it?"

"Mrs Lewis has stipulated in the will that should you marry again, ninety-nine per cent of the whole of the estate goes to the San Francisco Institute for Cripples." Weidman smiled his professional smile. "But I don't suppose, Mr Lewis, you contemplate marrying again?"

Harry sat for a long moment, scarcely believing what he had been told. Then he felt a cold rush of blood up his spine. His emotional feelings for Lisa went away like a smear wiped off a wall.

"Does that mean I can't ever marry again?" he asked, his voice husky.

"Why, of course you can, Mr Lewis." It was at this moment that Harry realised that Weidman disliked him as much as he disliked Weidman. "Naturally, you are free to do whatever you wish. However, if you do marry again, you then are left with the Florida Development Trust which, I believe, you are now handling and the rest of the estate – all of the estate, Mr Lewis – goes to the Institute."

"Are you serious?" Harry demanded. "Are you telling me I can never marry again without losing all the estate?"

"That is correct."

"But this is damnable!" Harry jumped to his feet. "Can't we fight it? It's inhuman!"

"Something like two hundred million dollars would be involved, Mr Lewis," Weidman said. "The Institute have very powerful, political backing. The terms of the will are explicit. Yes, of course, we could attempt to fight it, but I very much doubt if we would succeed." He regarded Harry, his shrewd eyes quizzing. "But at the moment, you don't wish to remarry?"

"Please go," Harry said and dropped into his chair. "I'll discuss this later."

When the Cadillac had driven away, Harry slammed his clenched fists together.

You bitch! he thought. You bloody minded, hateful cripple! So you've fixed me! You've condemned me to a life of mistresses! No children! So you deserved what you got! You bitch! You deserved to have the terror of such a death!

He hid his face in his hands and began to sob, his body shaking, uncontrolled, his nerves broken by the horror of this day.

Steve Harmas, Chief Investigator of a group of investigators working for the National Fidelity Insurance Co., wandered into Patty Shaw's office. He was a tall, ugly-looking man with a cheerful grin and a needle sharp brain.

Patty Shaw, Maddox's secretary, paused in her typing. Blonde and pretty, she was generally liked by all the male staff. She was not only smart, but helpful. Harmas claimed, second to his wife, she was his favourite woman.

"Hi," he said, coming to rest at her desk. "What's cooking?"

Patty flicked her fingers at Maddox's office door.

"He's been screaming for you for the past half-hour."

Harmas grimaced.

"What's eating him then? It's not yet ten o'clock."

"What you don't seem ever to remember is he's always at his desk at eight o'clock."

"Can I help it if he is crazy? So he wants me?"

"An understatement. You'd better take your anti-bear bite ointment in with you. He's acting as if a hornet has goosed him."

"Miss Shaw! What a way to talk!" Harmas grinned, crossed the room, tapped on Maddox's door and entered.

As usual, Maddox was crouched over his desk which was littered with papers, policies and letters. His thinning grey hair was rumpled and his red face was screwed into a scowl. Maddox wasn't a big man although he looked big from behind the shelter of his desk. He had the shoulders of a boxer and the legs of a midget. His eyes were cold, ruthless and restless. He wore his expensive suit anyhow. Cigarette ash rained down on his short front and his coat sleeves. He had a habit of constantly running his stubby fingers through his hair which added to his dishevelled appearance.

"I've been waiting for you!" he barked, sitting back in his desk chair. "It's ten o'clock! Don't you ever do any work around here?"

Harmas folded himself into a chair and lit a cigarette.

"I was on that Johnson drag until two this morning," he said. "My wife insists I get some sleep."

Maddox snorted. Regarded as the best and most brilliant claims assessor in the insurance business, he was aware of his position and drove his investigators hard, although he didn't cut any ice with Harmas who was also regarded as the best investigator in the business and who believed in taking life as easily as he could.

"Seen this?"

Maddox tossed a Telex over to Harmas.

"What's up now?"

"Read it!"

Harmas read the Telex from Alan Frisby, their agent in

143

Paradise City. As he read, he slowly sat upright. The lethargic expression on his face changed to alertness.

"Well, for crying out loud!" he exclaimed, dropping the Telex on the desk. "The Esmaldi diamonds! How the hell could they have got at them from a Raysons' safe?"

"They got at them!" Maddox said grimly. "This is going to set us back three hundred and fifty thousand unless we find them. I want you to go down there right away. This is a calculated, cleverly planned steal. Three of Raysons' safes have been opened. We don't have to worry about the Lowensteins' nor the Jacksons' steals ... we don't cover them. The steal forms a pattern. Talk to Hacket first. See what explanation he has to offer. We made a deal with Mrs Lewis to reduce her premium if she kept the necklace in her safe because we knew the safe was burglar proof. Yet someone has opened it. Someone who must have known how to turn off the hidden alarm. Who is this someone? They have a good police chief down there ... Terrell, but this is out of his class. I want you to work with him, and dig, and keep digging. I'm not paying out until I am sure I have to, so you have to work fast. Any moment I'll be saddled with a claim for this necklace. I'm not paying unless I damn well have to and if I have to, you'll be sorry!"

Harmas kept his face straight and nodded gravely. He had had this threat thrown at him so often it had become a joke. He wasn't scared of Maddox, but he let Maddox imagine he was.

"Okay," he said and climbed out of his chair. "Any suggestions?"

Maddox ran his fingers through his hair.

"Until I know different," he said, "there are only two outsiders who know how to open those safes: David Hacket and the man who fitted the safe."

"How about Hacket's secretary who must have access to his files?"

Maddox nodded.

"That's right. A boy-friend could have got at her.

You're thinking on the right lines. All these people must be put under a microscope, but I don't really dig for this. To me, this smells like a professional job. No fingerprints: no clues. Even if an amateur found out how to open the safes, how did he break into the houses without leaving a trace? All the same, Steve, you have to check these people. I still think this is an operation by a clever jewel gang who somehow have got hold of inside information."

"Could be one of them played up to Hacket's secretary and got the information out of her? You don't really think Hacket himself did the job?"

"Why not? Everyone of these people I've mentioned are suspects," Maddox growled. "The total take is close on a million dollars."

"But the Esmaldi necklace," Harmas said thoughtfully. "How do you sell a necklace as well known as that? Do you think they will break it up?"

"If they did, it would lose half its value. Could be they have found a crooked private dealer or a crazy collector. I don't know ... could be that."

"Well, okay, I'll get down there and I'll call you when I have found something."

"Two other points for you to keep in mind," Maddox said. "The woman's been murdered. The husband comes into all her money. Let's be sure this isn't a smoke screen to cover her killing." Seeing Harmas' startled expression, Maddox went on, "Oh, I know. Sounds crazy, but I've known husbands who have set the stage to look like robbery and then murdered their wives. Keep your eye on Lewis. The second point is tell Terrell to check over the fences in the district. There's Abe Schulman and Bernie Baum in Miami. Get him to put those two punks through the wringer."

"Okay."

Harmas left the office and paused by Patty's desk.

"Envy me," he said, smiling at her. "I'm off to Paradise City."

Patty rolled her big eyes.

"Lucky you. Be good, Steve ... remember you're a married man."

Harmas grinned.

"No chance of forgetting it. See you ... " and he left her, moving swiftly, taking the stairs down to the ground level two at a time. He drove home to collect a suitcase.

Captain Terrell shifted back in his chair and reached for his carton of coffee. Sitting opposite him was Sergeant Hess of Homicide and Sergeant Joe Beigler, a big, freckled-faced man who was Terrell's top sergeant.

"Well, we've certainly got a mess in our laps," Terrell said. "This is an organised gang steal, plus murder."

"What foxes me is that the Raysons' safes are supposed to be burglar proof," Beigler said, lighting a cigarette. He was seldom without a cigarette in his mouth. "They are burglar proof unless someone finds out how they operate, then they are dead easy. The Raysons people keep a strict security. So ... we now have the staff at Raysons as possible suspects. There's Hacket, the sales manager, Joleson who fits the safes and Hacket's secretary, Dina Lowes, who had access to the files. Any one of them could have done the job or sold their information to a gang who might have done the job. We've already checked on Joleson: he's on vacation on a cruise, but he could have sold the information. Hacket was at the Country Club until two o'clock and then went home with his wife. But he too could have sold the information. Miss Lowes has a boy-friend who she wants to marry. We've checked him ... seems okay, but she could have accepted a big bribe so they could get married fast."

There came a tap on the door and Detective Second Grade Tom Lepski came in. Lepski was one of Terrell's best detectives: a tall, wiry man regarded by his colleagues as a bit of a hellion, always kicking against discipline, but first-class in his job.

"I've got a lead, Chief," he said, coming to rest before

Terrell's desk. His thin, hawk-like face was animated. "Our first important break. There are eighteen Raysons' safes in this City and I've been checking every one of them."

Terrell waved to a chair.

"Sit down, Tom ... have some coffee."

Beigler, a coffee addict, poured some into a spare paper cup.

"I visited Warren Crail's house," Lepski said, reaching for one of Beigler's cigarettes. "That was my fifth call. I was asking if there had been anyone calling who wasn't in the picture ... some stranger asking questions. The housekeeper there is sharp. She told me a girl had called from the Acme Carpet Cleaning Co., saying Mrs Crail wanted an estimate for cleaning her carpets. The housekeeper wouldn't let the girl in. This sounded to me like a possible gag so I checked the phone book ... no Acme Carpet Cleaning Co. I drove over to Mrs Lowenstein's place. The butler tells me that a girl from this carpet cleaning firm called and he let her in. She measured the carpet in the room where the safe is. So I checked with Mrs Jackson's caretaker ... the same girl's been there." He flicked open his notebook. "Here's her description: slightly built, black hair, wearing heavy sun-goggles she didn't once take off, age around twenty-five, possibly younger, dressed in a blue frock with white collar and cuffs." Lepski closed his notebook. "The description doesn't vary: the housekeeper, the butler and the caretaker all gave the same exact description ... and here's the important lead: they all say the girl was driving a white Opel car, but none of them, of course, got the licence number." Lepski sat back and regarded Terrell, obviously waiting for praise.

"Nice work, Tom," Terrell said automatically. "This girl must be one of the gang. Right, at least, we now have something to work on. We're not giving this to the press. Could be the gang is still here. If we give a description of the girl, they could bolt. We have to find this white Opel.

I want the names and addresses of every owner of this type of car in the district and don't forget the hire car services. That's our first move." He was now talking to Hess. "Get four or five of your men on this right away, Fred. There can't be all that number of white Opels in the City, but to make sure, we'll call the Miami police and rope them in. This gang might be operating from Miami."

Hess nodded and left the office.

Terrell thought for a long moment.

"I don't see what we can do about this girl for the moment. At least we know there's a young girl with this gang. Tom, I want you to go to all the real estate agents and find out if any villa has been let within the past month and if rented by a group of people, one of them a girl around twenty-five. This is a long shot, but it could pay off. Then I want some of our men to check all the hotels. I want a list of those people who haven't been in Paradise City before. The hotel will know their regulars. Check with the hotel dicks."

Lepski got to his feet.

"Okay, Chief," he said, and leaving Terrell and Beigler together, he went down the stairs to his car.

CHAPTER SEVEN

None of the four moved until they heard Abe's car drive away, then Johnny reached for a cigarette. He had told Abe he had been to the Casino the previous night and had lost five thousand of Abe's dollars. Abe knew this to be a lie, but he was stuck with it. He was anxious to get most of his money back and get away from the villa, he had to accept the lie. He had gone off with ninety-five thousand dollars, and he reckoned himself lucky to have got even that amount.

"Don't let's get excited," Johnny said quietly. "Let's see how much money we have left. I have Abe's five thousand," He looked at Henry. "Colonel?"

Henry hesitated, then lifted his old, drooping shoulders.

"Five hundred."

"Gilda?"

"Me?" She waved her hands helplessly. "Twenty dollars."

"Fatso ... what have you left?"

"You call me Fatso, you murdering sonofabitch, and I'll cut your throat!"

"Never mind my throat ... how much have you got?"

"Listen to me, you creep!" Martha's face turned purple. "I financed this plan. I've already spent more than five thousand dollars to set it up. Now ... what have we got? Nothing! And why? Because I was stupid enough to hook up with a vicious killer like you!"

"I didn't ask for a commentary," Johnny said quietly. "How much have you got?"

"Nothing! Whatever I have left, I'm keeping for myself!"

Johnny shrugged.

"Okay. So you have nothing, you greedy old liar. Well, at least we have five thousand and the Cadillac. I'll sell the car. I'll get four thousand for it. So that gives us nine thousand. We can live on that for two more weeks and have something to spare." He pointed to the brief-case on the table. "And we have the jewels."

"Are you crazy?" Martha screamed, slamming her fat fist down on the table. "You heard what that rat said ... that stuff is dynamite!"

Johnny regarded her, his expression calm, his eyes mocking.

"Yes, it's dynamite now, but in a couple of years, I could do a deal with it. The heat will be off and we could sell the stuff. We'll have to wait. Two years and we're where we came in."

Listening to this, Henry nodded.

"He's right, Martha. In less than two years, I could sell this stuff to Milkes in New York. He would take it. Maybe we wouldn't get more than a quarter of its value, but a quarter is better than nothing."

Martha drew in a long, slow breath, her bosom heaving.

"What are we going to do with it now?" she asked.

"I'll stash it away in a safe deposit box at the airport," Johnny said. "I'll do it right away and then sell the Caddy. We'll keep the Opel. But first we have to clean up. There's my shirt ... there's Gilda's wig and the office dress. By now the cops will know all about the Acme Carpet Cleaning Co. Come on," he was now speaking to Gilda. "We'll put the lot in the barbecue and make a bonfire."

An hour later, the bloodstained shirt, Gilda's wig, her dress and sun-goggles were ashes in the outdoor barbecue.

Johnny picked up the brief-case.

"You two take it easy," he said. "I'll stash this away and

get rid of the Caddy." He looked at Gilda. "Do you want to come with me?"

She nodded and followed him down to the Cadillac, parked in the sun.

As he was driving down the beach road, Gilda said, "I knew it was too good to be true . . . it was all too easy. I knew it."

Johnny glanced at her, then shrugged.

"It'll work out. We won't make so much money, but if we're patient we can still pick up enough."

"You mean . . . enough for your garage?"

"That's it."

"That's all you think about, isn't it?"

"What else is there to think about? I want that garage, and I'm going to have it!"

Gilda looked down at her hands.

"Martha and Henry mean nothing to you, do they?"

Johnny shifted in the driving seat, frowning.

"Must you talk this way? No . . . they mean nothing to me. That fat old bitch . . . and Henry . . . he's as good as dead . . . why should they mean anything to me?"

"And me? Still nothing?"

Johnny gave an exasperated sigh.

"You're all mixed up," he said after a long pause. "You won't remember me in six months' time. There have been other girls in my life and they all had a thing about me . . . don't ask me why. When I ran into them after a few months, they didn't even recognise me."

Gilda looked out of the car window. The sea and the sand and the people enjoying themselves on the beach were a tear-misted blur of colour.

"That must have been nice for you," she said bitterly.

Johnny looked at her. Women! he thought.

An hour later, they came out of the Florida Safe Deposit Bank at the airport, having rented a safe in the name of Paul Whitney with a faked Los Angeles address. The brief-case was stashed away in one of the many safe deposit boxes and Johnny was satisfied the jewels were now safe.

"Now we'll get rid of the car."

Gilda stood around while Johnny haggled with the second-hand car salesman. The haggling was long and bitter, but finally, Johnny got the price he wanted: four thousand dollars. He put the roll of money in his hip pocket and joined Gilda.

"Well, we're set," he said. "All we have to do is to sit tight and bluff it out. We're in the clear."

Gilda walked with him across the road to a taxi rank.

"How will we survive for two years?" she asked.

"At the end of our lease, we leave," Johnny said. "We'll all go to Miami. I'll dig up something. Martha will get ideas ... fat as she is, she's no fool. We'll have to live tight until the heat is off, then we pick up the jewels and we're in the money."

Gilda looked searchingly at him.

"Then you are going to stay with us ... remain with us?"

Johnny grinned.

"What do you think? I want my share of the pay-off. Sure, we're all going to stick together until we can sell that stuff."

Gilda drew in a long, deep breath. Maybe, she thought, in those future months, Johnny might come to care for her.

David Hacket, the sales manager of Raysons' safes, was preparing to close the office and go home when Steve Harmas walked in. Although he had never met Harmas, Hacket had heard of him: the best insurance investigator in the business. He was pleased and thankful to see Harmas.

Dina Lowes, Hacket's secretary, a smart, good-looking girl, brought Harmas into Hacket's well appointed office.

"Okay, Dina, you get off," Hacket said after he had

shaken hands with Harmas. "Lock the outer door. I have my key."

When his secretary had gone, Hacket waved Harmas to a seat and sat down beside his desk.

Hacket was tall and immaculately dressed: a man of thirty-eight years of age: handsome with clear grey eyes that held Harmas in a steady, level gaze. Harmas immediately liked him as all those who met him liked him.

"Glad to have you here, Harmas," Hacket said as they settled in their chairs. "This is a mess. I realise I could be suspect number one. I bet Maddox has told you to dig into my private life and into Dina's too."

Harmas gave his lazy, cheerful grin.

"His very words. What is killing him is how anyone could open a Raysons' safe. Up to now, we have looked on your safes as the best insurance bet of all safes, and yet, three of them have been opened and cleaned out."

Hacket spread his hands.

"Don't imagine Maddox is the only one. I have had Head Office screaming at me. I just don't know how it happened. So I am suspect number one." He shrugged. "Our security is really tight. I'll swear by Dina. Joleson, our fitter, has been with us for twenty-three years. I'll swear by him." He gave a crooked smile. "I'll even swear by myself ... so somehow, this gang has got hold of the blueprints of the various safes. How they did it, I can't imagine."

Harmas stroked his nose.

"Where do you keep the blueprints?"

"In that cabinet there." Hacket pointed to the filing cabinet against the far wall.

Harmas levered himself out of his chair and examined the lock of the cabinet.

"That lock doesn't mean much," Hacket said. "But we are wired all over. Anyone entering this office breaks a ray and the police are alerted. Anyone touching that cabinet sets off an alarm. This office is really protected, Harmas, make no mistake about that."

"Is the alarm on now?"

"No, I'll put it on when I leave."

"Could you have forgotten to put it on at any time?"

"No. This is routine to me. It's like when I shave in the morning. This is something I don't forget to do."

"What happens if there is an electricity cut?"

"We have our own generator."

"Could your generator get tampered with?"

Hacket looked startled.

"I don't think so. It's down in the basement. The janitor has strict instructions not to let anyone down there."

Harmas moved around the office while he thought.

"Someone has got at your files," he said after some moments. "This must mean they have tampered with your generator. What I want from you is a list of everyone who has been here in your office during the past month. Do you keep a record?"

"Sure."

"Fine . . . get me out a list. I want the names of everyone who has been here. Will you do that."

"It'll be ready for you first thing tomorrow."

When Harmas left the office, he took the elevator down to the basement and talked to the janitor.

An hour later he walked up the worn steps leading to the Paradise City's police headquarters.

Charlie Tanner, the desk sergeant, was about to leave for home. He regarded Harmas with his cold, cop stare.

"The Chief in?" Harmas asked, coming to rest before Tanner's desk.

"Yeah, but he's busy."

"So am I," Harmas said with his easy smile. "Tell him Harmas of the National Fidelity Insurance Co. I want to see him."

Tanner reached for a telephone, spoke into it, then jerked his thumb to a flight of stairs.

"That's the way."

Harmas found Terrell going through a mass of reports. Sergeant Joe Beigler, a cigarette between his lips, a carton of coffee by his side, was also reading reports.

Harmas introduced himself and Terrell got out of his chair to shake hands. He had heard of Harmas' reputation and of Maddox's brilliance.

"Glad to have you here," Terrell said. "Have some coffee?"

Harmas shook his head. He settled himself on the hard upright chair.

"Maddox sent me down in case I could help," he explained. "What do you make of it so far?"

Terrell leaned his massive body back in his chair.

"This is a clever, well organised steal. The gang obviously had inside information. They must have got at Raysons' blueprints to have opened those safes. It is possible they could have done the Lowensteins' and the Jacksons' steals some days or even some weeks before they did the Lewis job. I think it's possible they got information that both Mrs Lowenstein and the Jacksons were out of town. They could have got this information from the local paper's gossip column. The Lewis job bothers me. This doesn't conform to pattern. The other two steals were neat. Whoever did the job knew both houses were only guarded by a servant. The Lewis steal is different. Whoever did that job must have known Mrs Lewis was in the room where the safe was. The murder was premeditated. I'm saying this because the killer took a bronze statue from the hall, climbed the stairs and brutally killed her with it. The fact he did this, rather than killing her with a weapon in the bedroom, points to deliberate intent to murder. This upsets the pattern of the other two jobs. Jewel thieves are seldom killers. So we have a set-up with the Lewis job that puzzles me."

Harmas nodded. What Terrell said made sense to him.

"I've been talking to Hacket," Harmas said. "You're right. This gang did get access to Hacket's blueprints. His office is protected as you know, but he has his own generator. I've talked to the janitor. He tells me ten days ago, an electrician wearing the uniform of the City's Electricity Co. called, saying there was a fault. The janitor let him have the run of the basement. I suggest you check on this and check the generator plant for fingerprints."

Terrell swung around in his chair.

"Joe, cover this! Send the fingerprint boys down to that basement right now!"

Beigler left the room with surprising swiftness for a man of his size.

"I have a feeling," Terrell went on, looking at Harmas, "that the Lewis job is divorced from the other two steals. I could be wrong because the three steals have the same professional touch. In each case there are no signs of how the thieves got into the house: all the locks are tricky. But in the Lewis case, a window was left open as if showing us how the thief broke in. This didn't happen with the other two steals."

"Maddox is thinking along the same lines," Harmas said. "He told me to take a look at Harry Lewis, the husband."

"We're taking a good look at him," Terrell said quietly. "I have two good men digging. The jewels taken from Mrs Lowenstein and from Mrs Jackson could be broken up, but the Esmaldi necklace would lose half its value if it was broken up. I'm now wondering if the Lewis steal should be considered as something separate."

Harmas stretched and suppressed a yawn.

"Yeah ... it's an idea. Well, Chief, I've had a long day. I'm going to relax. You can find me at the Plaza Hotel if you want me. I'll keep in touch."

But when Harmas left police headquarters, he drove to Alan Frisby's home, knowing Frisby, at this time, would have left his office.

As the National Fidelity Insurance district agent, Frisby was pleased to welcome Harmas. He introduced him to his wife, Janet, and to his seven-year-old twin sons, then he led Harmas out on to the terrace and the men sat down.

Janet, a nice-looking brunette, said she would put the twins to bed and then they would all have supper on the terrace.

While she was busy, Harmas and Frisby discussed the robberies.

"This gang is well organised," Harmas said. "What interests me is how they knew where to find the jewels. Their field work is impressive. They knew Mrs Lowenstein was in a clinic otherwise the girl wouldn't have called on the house, claiming Mrs L. had asked for an estimate. That goes for Mrs Jackson's place too."

"They could have got their information from the local rag," Frisby said.

"I have an idea they have been collecting information from Raysons and from you without either of you knowing it. What I want you to do is to let me have a list of the names of everyone who has visited your office over the past four weeks."

"Nothing simpler. We always keep a log of everyone coming to us, but I think you are wasting your time."

Harmas smiled.

"Maddox would love to hear that remark. He is firmly convinced I never do anything else except waste time."

Harry Lewis sat in his study.

He was listening to the heavy tramp of the undertakers' feet as they went to Lisa's room. Each footfall made him flinch. Then there was a long silence and he imagined these men lifting the disfigured dead body from the bed to the coffin. He clenched his fists. But he could feel no pity for Lisa. She had condemned him now to live alone. All she had left him was money.

He listened to the heavy tread as they brought the coffin down and the whispered words of caution as the men manoeuvred the coffin around the sharp bend of the staircase, and then finally the snap of the doors of the hearse as they closed.

Well, now she is gone, he thought, reaching for his glass. He had been drinking steadily since he had returned to this big, luxury house which was now his. He listened as the hearse drove away. He was free of her, yet he wasn't free of her. He would have to get rid of this house. He couldn't continue to live in it. He would have to get rid of the staff. He would have to make a new life for himself.

Tania! Would she accept the position of his mistress? He remembered what she had said to him: *If anything happens to her, would you marry me?* He rubbed his hand wearily across his face. He would have to be very careful how he explained the situation to her. With his sudden enormous wealth, he could give her everything she wanted except marriage and a position in Paradise City's society. He knew he dare not live openly in sin with her. The Yacht Club, the English Club, the narrow minded rich who he now would mix with wouldn't stand for him living with a Vietnamese waitress, no matter how much money he had ... they wouldn't take that.

He leaned back in his chair, thinking. Maybe it was better after all not to be in a position to marry Tania. He wanted to keep in with Lisa's friends. A Vietnamese ... no, maybe it was for the best, but he couldn't bear the thought of losing her. She was in his blood like a virus. He would explain tactfully and he was sure she would understand.

He looked at his watch. It was now after eight o'clock. He decided he would go to the Saigon Restaurant. He had had no lunch, but even now he wasn't hungry, but he could talk to Tania. He had to talk to her.

As he got to his feet, he realised he was free to go to her. No more sneaking out at night. No one to check on him. In a few days, once the will was settled, he would get rid of the staff, sell the house and look for something smaller where he could lead a bachelor's life.

As he walked through the hall, To-To appeared.

"I'm dining out," Harry said curtly and went down to the garage without looking at To-To.

Dong Tho welcomed him with a low bow, his yellow face grave. He took him through the noisy bustle of the restaurant to the private room. He said nothing about Lisa, but the way he behaved, his low bows, conveyed to Harry his distress and sympathy.

"I'll have soup ... nothing else," Harry said, sitting at the table. "Is Tania here?"

"I will send her to you, Mr Lewis."

Harry lit a cigarette and stared bleakly out of the window, realising how nervous he was.

A waiter brought the soup. Harry guessed that Tania would wait until he had finished his meal before coming to the room. When he had finished the soup, he pushed away the bowl and relaxed, watching the tourists on the quay.

The door opened and Tania came in. She was wearing a white tunic over black trousers. She wore no make-up and there were dark smudges under her eyes. She paused as she closed the door. They looked at each other, then she came and sat down opposite him.

"I heard it on the radio," she said softly. "I wanted to telephone, but I thought I had better not. This is a terrible thing, Harry."

He nodded.

"You remember what I said ... about destiny?" she went on. "I lit a candle for her."

Again Harry nodded. He was watching her, aware that he could read nothing from her expression of her feelings. Even the almond-shaped eyes told him nothing.

"You are free now," she said after a long pause.

"Yes."

They regarded each other, then she sensed his uneasiness and she leaned forward, her small slim hands resting on the tablecloth.

"You are free, Harry?"

159

Harry hesitated, then without looking at the beautiful, Oriental face, he said, "I have all her money ... everything she owned, but I'm not really free."

He saw her hands turn into fists.

"What does that mean please?"

Again Harry hesitated. She may as well know now, he thought. She has to know sooner or later.

"There's a clause in the will ... " He forced himself to face her. They sat motionless, staring at each other. Tania's face had hardened. It was as if the muscles under her skin had turned to stone. He scarcely knew her now and her black eyes seemed to have turned to glass.

"What clause?" she asked.

"I lose everything if I marry again. Everything will go to a cripples' home."

Tania remained motionless: her hands into fists, her eyes blank. She said nothing.

With an unsteady hand, Harry stubbed out his cigarette.

"I'm sorry, darling," he said finally. "She has been a bitch to the end. But now I have all the money I could ever need. There is nothing you can't have ... "

"Thank you. I see, but I am to remain your whore?"

Harry reached for her hands, but she snatched them away, dropping them into her lap.

"Don't talk like that, Tania," he pleaded. "I can do so much for you now, but I can't do anything for you if we married. You must understand."

"What can you do for me?" she demanded.

"Ask ... anything. You can have a beautiful house ... you can furnish it just as you like. Any car you want ... jewels ... clothes ... there's nothing I can't give you."

"But I can't become your wife?"

Harry spread his hands.

"No."

"I can't meet your friends? I'm to remain a whore?"

"Tania! You know how much I love you ... you're hurting me talking this way."

160

"Truth often hurts."

Harry lit another cigarette. Was he going to lose her? he wondered. He was sick with anxiety.

"Please try to understand, darling," he said. "Please . . ."

She lifted her shoulders.

"I will try to understand. I must think about it." She got to her feet. "Please keep away from me for a few days." She went out of the room.

Harry sat for a long time, staring blankly out at the quay. Then, with an effort, he got to his feet and walked into the busy restaurant. He gave the smiling waiter a ten dollar tip. As he moved to the main exit, Dong Tho came out of the shadows.

"Please be patient with her, Mr Lewis," he said, bowing. "She is very young and still romantic."

Harry nodded and went out to where his car was parked.

Johnny woke with a start. He had gone to bed early, leaving Martha and Henry on the terrace and Gilda glued to the TV set. He wanted to be alone. The knowledge that he would have to wait two years before he got his garage irked him. He felt pretty sure the garage in Carmel would be sold before he could afford to put in a bid, so he would have to shop around for something else. But he knew he had to be patient. Anything done in a hurry now would be fatal.

Eventually, still hearing Martha talking on the terrace and the sound of the TV set, he drifted off into an uneasy sleep. Now he was awake and he became aware that his bedroom door was softly opening.

The window was open and the moonlight made a puddle of silver on the carpet. He looked at the face of his watch: the time was just after two o'clock.

He waited, tense, ready to spring out of bed, then he relaxed as Gilda came silently into the room.

"Are you awake?"

"Yes ... what is it?"

He lay still, watching her as she moved to the bed and sat on the edge of it. She was wearing a white wrap which she held closely to her.

"I wanted to talk to you."

He reached for the bedside lamp, but paused as she raised her hand.

"No, please ... "

He regarded her, then shrugged.

"You shouldn't be here ... what is it?"

"I'm scared, Johnny."

"Why?"

"I have a feeling we're in a trap ... Martha feels the same way."

"That fat old bitch ... "

"She feels it ... and Henry too. They're relying on you now, Johnny ... so am I."

"Oh, for God's sake! We are taking a risk, but we'll get away with it," Johnny said irritably. "They can't prove anything even if they find us. It's just a matter of keeping our nerve."

"I wish I could feel like you do."

"I can't stiffen your spine ... that's up to you."

"You don't care for anyone but yourself, do you, Johnny?"

"Why the hell should I? Don't let's go over all that again!"

"No, I'm sorry." She sat still, her hands in her lap. The moonlight lit her hair, putting her face in a shadow. She looked very beautiful as she stared down at him. "You see, Johnny, I've been thinking. I love you. I feel sure we are coming to the end of our road. Something bad is going to happen to us all. I know you don't love me, but I do want something to remember you by ... please make love to me."

"Something bad? What the hell do you mean?"

"Does it matter?" She stood up and dropped the wrap from her. "I'm offering myself to you."

He stared at her naked body, the moonlight striking across her breasts.

"You'd better get out of here," he said harshly. "Go on ... beat it! I've done some rotten things in my life, but I'm not going to kid you ... get out!"

She moved to him, slid down beside him and put her arms around him.

"Just for me to remember you by, Johnny," she said softly. "Please ... "

For a moment he resisted the feel of her yielding flesh, then he pulled her roughly to him.

Captain Terrell was reading through a mass of reports he had found waiting for him when he arrived at his office. The time now was half-past ten and he was reaching for his third carton of coffee when Steve Harmas came in.

"Hi, Chief," Harmas said, dropping on to an upright chair. "How's it going?"

"Working on this white Opel car," Terrell said, and grimaced. "Believe it or not there are two hundred and three registered white Opels in this district and fifteen registered with Hertz. Looks like a long slog to check them all."

"I can save you a little work," Harmas said. "Look at the Hertz list. Got a Colonel Shelley down there?"

Terrell stared at him, then picked up the list. He scanned it, then nodded.

"Yeah ... Colonel Shelley of Villa Bellevue hired a white Opel on 27th August."

Harmas grinned happily.

"We're getting hot."

"Bellevue ... that's Jack Carson's place. He rents it out at $1,500 a month."

"Could be our people. I got Frisby, our agent, and Hacket to give me a list of people who visited them during the past four weeks," Harmas said, lighting a cigarette. "On both lists up comes Colonel and Mrs Shelley. Now, they have hired a white Opel. I like the look of it."

Terrell scratched the side of his jaw as he thought.

"I'd better get a couple of my men over there and have them take a look at them."

Harmas shook his head.

"Don't let's rush this, Chief. I'll call Maddox. He knows all the jewel thieves of any account the way you know the top of your desk. Mrs Shelley is fat. Both Frisby and Hacket tell me she's the fattest woman they have ever seen. Let's see what Maddox says first."

Terrell waved to the telephone.

"Call him."

It took only five minutes to get through to Maddox.

"I have a big, fat woman who could be a suspect," Harmas said. "Does that jell? Big and really fat, around fifty-five, blonde. She's with a man who calls himself Colonel Shelley: looks like an aged stork: full of old Kentucky manners."

"That's Fats Gummrich and Jasie the Duke," Maddox said promptly. "Ha! This job's right up that fat old cow's alley! I'll send you their photos, Steve. Meet the three o'clock plane. Nice work."

"We haven't a shred of proof," Harmas said.

"Then get some!" Maddox barked and hung up.

Harmas winced and replaced the receiver.

"He knows them," he said to Terrell. "We get their photos on the three o'clock plane." He went on to tell Terrell what Maddox had said. "Better wait until we get the photos, huh?"

Terrell nodded.

"But with the photos we still haven't got anything on them."

"Did anything come out of my idea to check the generator for prints?"

"I'm waiting. We got a mass of prints. They've gone to Washington. I should hear any time now." Terrell reached for his telephone and called Hess. "Fred? Heard anything from Washington yet?"

"No, Chief. If they turn up anything, they said they would call back right away."

Terrell grunted and replaced the receiver.

"We'll have to wait."

Harmas climbed lazily to his feet.

"I guess I'll take a look at your City. I'll pick up the photos at three and then come over here. Okay?"

"Do that," Terrell said.

The morning passed quickly for Harmas. He returned to his hotel, put on a pair of swimming trunks and went down to the beach. He believed in relaxing. If Maddox had seen him, lying under a sun umbrella, watching the various girls in their skimpy bikinis disporting themselves in the sea, he would have had a coronary. Harmas was happy. He had an instinctive feeling that he was going to break this case and he saw no point now in exerting himself. He picked up with a gay, nice-looking blonde and they had lunch together. It was strictly platonic although Harmas got the idea that it could cease to be at the slightest encouragement from him, but dutifully faithful to his wife who he adored, he restrained himself.

He drove to the airport, arriving there as the 'Frisco plane touched down. He accepted the envelope the air hostess gave him and paused to flirt with her harmlessly. Pretty girls were his weakness up to a certain point. He then drove to Raysons' Safe Co. and showed Hacket the two photographs.

Hacket took one look and nodded.

"That's them. Who are they?"

"According to Maddox, she is Fats Gummrich and he is Jasie the Duke . . . both smart jewel thieves."

"So you think they got at my files?"

"Looks like it, doesn't it?"

Hacket raised his hands helplessly.

"My boss will love that!"

"Take it easy . . . could have happened to anyone."

Harmas next drove to Alan Frisby's office and got him

also to identify the photographs, then satisfied, he drove to police headquarters.

"There they are," he said, dropping the two photos on Terrell's desk. "Both Hacket and Frisby identify them. Now we have to dig up some evidence against them."

"I've dug up something," Terrell said with satisfaction. "We've just had a call from Washington. Fingerprints found on the generator belong to a guy named Johnny Robins." He went on to give Harmas a brief outline of Johnny's background. "Known to be violent," he concluded. "I've had a check on Hertz car rentals. They say the Opel was taken away by a man answering Robins' description. I've checked the Real Estate agent who let Bellevue to the Shelleys. He has given the same description of their chauffeur."

"Still isn't proof," Harmas said.

"That's right. We now have to take a chance. I have obtained a search warrant. We'll go there right away and take the villa to pieces. With any luck we might find something to nail them with."

"And if you don't find anything?"

"We have enough to arrest Robins and we'll bring him here and work him over. He could crack." Terrell got up.

"Mind if I come along?"

"Sure. Glad to have you."

Harmas followed Terrell out into the passage where Hess, Beigler and Lepski were waiting. Six uniformed officers were already in a car, waiting in the police car park.

Johnny swam around Gilda as she floated on her back, staring up at the blueness of the sky, feeling the heat of the sun on her face, her hands moving lazily to keep her balance.

Johnny trod water, coming close to her. Feeling he was gazing at her, she looked at him and smiled.

Their night together had been a success. At first, he had

taken her brutally, hurting her. Then later, in the small hours of the morning, as the red rim of the sun crept over the horizon, he had taken her as she had hoped he might take her. His slow, gentle thrusts into her had given her the pleasure she had so often thought could happen to her but up to now hadn't experienced. When it was over, Johnny had drawn her to him, enfolding her with a tenderness that she could scarcely believe.

And now, swimming together, she felt confident. She was sure she had done the right thing by giving herself to him. There was a new look in Johnny's eyes as they smiled at each other.

"Let's go back," Johnny said. "Two hours before dinner ... I want you."

She put her wet hand on his shoulder.

"I want you too."

They swam slowly side by side and when they reached the beach, they walked across the sand, hand in hand. Gilda's white bikini was plastered to her body and Johnny looked at her, feeling the urge to make love to her right there on the hot sand, his grip on her hand hurt her, but she didn't mind. She read his thoughts and returned his pressure.

"Let's hurry," she said and breaking away from him, she ran up the steps, shaking her wet hair, and reached the terrace. Then she stopped short, her heart missing a beat as she saw four men sitting stiffly on bamboo chairs, facing Martha. Behind them stood five police officers, relaxed but very alert, leaning against the terrace rail.

She felt Johnny's hand on her spine and she shuddered. He pushed her gently aside and walked across the terrace until he reached Martha who was sitting solid, like an enormous lump of inanimated flesh, staring at Captain Terrell like a rabbit facing a ferret.

"What goes on?" Johnny asked calmly.

Gaining courage from Johnny's manner, Henry said, "There's some mistake ... these gentlemen are police officers." He waved his old, freckled hand.

"You Johnny Robins?" Terrell asked, getting to his feet.

"That's my name," Johnny said quietly.

"We have reason to believe you and these others are connected with the inquiries we are making concerning the Lowenstein and the Jackson jewel robberies and also Mrs Lewis's murder," Terrell said. "We have a search warrant. Have you anything to say?"

Johnny walked over to where a towel was hanging over the back of a chair. He began to dry himself.

"I've no idea what you're talking about. As the Colonel has said ... there must be some mistake."

Terrell looked at Gilda, standing petrified, her face chalk white. "You anything to say?"

She tried to control her terror.

"N-no."

Hess came out on to the terrace. His hard eyes gleamed with triumph.

"You!" He pointed a stubby finger at Johnny. "Your room the third on the left down the corridor?"

Johnny stiffened, feeling a sudden cold rush of blood down his spine.

"Yes ... so what?"

"Come with me," Hess said. "I've something to show you."

Now uneasy, now a little scared, Johnny walked with Hess across the big living-room, down the corridor and into his bedroom.

"I left it as I found it," Hess said. "Now you tell me you've never seen it before."

There was a hard-faced cop, holding one of Johnny's jackets. From the pocket, he took a three string rope of pearls.

"Yours?" Hess barked.

Johnny stared at the necklace, feeling the blood draining out of his face. He had completely forgotten that he had taken it from Abe Schulman as "treachery" money and had kept it as he had told Martha as "danger" money.

He was quick to recover from the shock, but not quick enough. Watching him, Hess saw the look of dismay and the loss of colour before Johnny's face became blank and sullen.

"I know nothing about that," Johnny said, aware his voice was husky. He cleared his throat, then went on, "You planted it on me."

"Tell that to the Judge," Hess sneered. "Oh, boy! Are you in trouble, you creep!"

Johnny now had his nerve back, but he realised it was a little late.

"Screw you," he said. "You planted that on me and you can't prove otherwise."

"Let's see what Fats says," Hess said and taking the pearl necklace from the officer, he walked past Johnny and out on to the terrace. He dropped the necklace on the table in front of Martha.

"Take a look at this," he said. "Okay, I know you didn't kill her, but if you don't come clean, Fats, we'll have you on an accessory rap and sister! will you go away for a long, long time!"

Martha recognised the necklace. Her fat face turned into a quivering jelly.

"He did it, the vicious sonofabitch!" she shrilled. "I knew nothing about it! He tried to gyp us! He went there and killed her and took the Esmaldi diamonds! We knew nothing about it . . . I swear we didn't!"

"Stop it!" Gilda screamed, rushing across the terrace. "Stop it, you horrible old woman! He didn't do it!"

Two police officers grabbed and held her.

Johnny came out on to the terrace. Sobbing, Gilda tried to go to him, but she was held back.

"Oh, Johnny . . . Johnny . . . I knew it!"

Martha and Henry went in the first police car. Gilda, still sobbing, went with Flo, the maid, in the second. Johnny, now handcuffed, went with Hess in the third.

Martha was quivering and she put her hand on Henry's arm for comfort.

"Have you that pill?" Henry asked, his lips scarcely moving.

Martha shook her head.

Henry shrugged. He pushed her hand away. He was suddenly not sure even if she had had the pill if he would have taken it. Perhaps not. It needed courage to end your life in cold blood, and at his age, Henry was running out of courage.

CHAPTER EIGHT

Al Barney wig-wagged with his eyebrows and Sam, the barman, came over with a pint of beer: this made Al's seventeenth pint since we had sat down together.

"Well now, mister," he said after he had refreshed himself. He wiped the froth off his mouth with the back of his hand. "For you to understand how this all worked out, I want to bring Felix Warren, the District Attorney of this city, on to the scene. As I've already told you, I have my ear to the ground, and from what I've picked up about Felix Warren, I've come to the conclusion that you couldn't find a more ambitious, ruthless sonofabitch in this fair city. And, let me tell you, when I look around at all these rich creeps who live here, showing off, throwing their money around and behaving as if they were the Almighty Himself, it beats me how Warren could lead them all, but that's just what he has done ... a real bitch-bastard, if you'll excuse the expression." Al eased himself down in his chair and went on, "It was stinking bad luck for Johnny that Warren was one of Lisa Lewis's few personal friends ... not that Warren liked her, mind you, but he had this thing about keeping in with everyone who was in the real money. As soon as her murder made the headlines, he held a press conference and told the reporters, who had always hated his guts, that he would leave no stone unturned to catch her killer ... that's the crummy way he talked ... no stone unturned. This bit of gas made as much impression on the newsmen as a lump of dough flung against a brick wall. Warren hadn't any sort of reputation. His term of office was coming to an end.

He had done nothing to make the electors want him back, but now he saw in Lisa Lewis's killing his big chance to put on a court room show that might gain him much needed votes."

He, Captain Terrell and the Assistant District Attorney sat down together around Warren's big desk.

This meeting took place three days after the arrest of the gang. During this time, Terrell's men and his Lab boys had been working around the clock. Now Terrell had a neatly summarised report which he laid before Warren.

Warren, heavily built, balding with moist stone-hard eyes, read the report, grunted, then dropped it on his desk and sat back.

"We've got him!" he declared.

Terrell regarded him.

"We have got *them* on the Lowenstein and the Jackson jobs," he said quietly, "but not on the Lewis killing. Mr District Attorney, I have always felt this is a separate job and should be dealt with as such."

Warren reacted as if he had been stung by a bee. He glared at Terrell.

"What are you talking about? Robins killed her! There's no question about it!"

"On the face of it," Terrell said, "it does look that way, but it won't stand up in court. Let's look at what we know: Robins was a Raysons' safe expert. He is vicious. He has a record. But he has put forward an alibi. He claims he was with this woman all night ... the night Mrs Lewis was killed. We've talked to this woman. She admits she joined Robins at this restaurant ... she says she wanted a light for a cigarette. She says they got talking. They left together and then she claims they parted outside the restaurant, but I am satisfied that she is lying. She had to go along with Robins' story up to this point because she's smart enough to know we could dig up twenty witnesses in the restaurant who saw her contact Robins. But no one saw her leave in her car, so no one can tell whether Robins was with her or not. This woman has an unsavoury reputation. As soon as her aged husband leaves for New York – which he does at least once a month – she is in bed with the first man she can grab."

Warren's well-fed face turned mauve.

"Are you talking about Mrs Helene Booth?" he rasped, leaning forward and glaring at Terrell. "I'll have you know Mrs Booth is a personal friend of mine, and what you have just said amounts to a damaging libel which could cost you your job! Let me tell you, Mrs Booth is a very fine woman, and I am astonished and ashamed that you have sent one of your men to put such questions to her. This is quite disgraceful, and I am astonished that a man of your experience could even think of accepting such a filthy alibi ... and that's what it is ... a filthy, unsupported alibi."

Terrell hesitated. He knew about Helene Booth and her nymphomania, but if she was the friend of the District Attorney, then he realised he had to play his cards carefully.

"I'm telling you what has been reported to me," he said woodenly.

"Then it's a damn lie!" Warren shouted, slamming his fist down on the desk. "Look at this man! Vicious! Served a sentence for attacking a police officer! A womaniser! Expert in locks! I'll hang this killing on him if it's the last thing I do!"

"But how?" Terrell asked. "If we had caught him with the Esmaldi necklace, we would have had a case, but the necklace has vanished. We've checked every safe deposit box in the city: we've checked everywhere ... no necklace."

"I don't give a goddamn about the necklace," Warren said. "He could have put it in the mail ... it could be anywhere. He was in a struggle with Mrs Lewis ... those scratches on his arms. He tried to burn his bloodstained shirt, but your men turned up enough evidence of the shirt to show the blood group matches Mrs Lewis's blood group."

"They also match his," Terrell pointed out.

Warren sat back. He squinted at Terrell, his eyes probing and hostile.

"Are you rooting for this thug, Terrell?" he demanded. "Sounds to me as if you are."

Terrell was too experienced to be fazed by this remark, but he warned himself he had to tread carefully.

"I'm not, but I'm warning you, Mr District Attorney, that with the kind of evidence we have so far against Robins, we won't be able to make a murder charge stick in court."

Warren rubbed his fleshy hand across his chin. He smiled: it was an evil smile.

"That's your opinion. I will now remind you that I am in charge of this case. I'll make it stick. I want to talk to this woman ... Gummrich ... here now in my office. Have her sent to me!"

A little over an hour later, a tall hatchet-faced policewoman brought Martha into Warren's impressive office. Warren flicked his fingers at the policewoman and told her to wait outside. When she had gone, he turned his attention to Martha who stood before him, quivering like a jelly, her eyes red rimmed with weeping and feeling unbearably hungry. The three days she had spent in a cell, eating the disgusting food served up by the prison authorities, had lowered her morale as nothing else could.

Warren looked her over. He disliked fat women. He thought Martha was disgusting to the eye, but he fixed on his face his famous, oily court-room smile and waved her to a chair.

"Mrs Gummrich? Sit down." He selected a Havana cigar from a cedar wood box and nipped its end with a gold cigar-cutter.

Martha flopped into a chair. Her small frightened eyes moved around the room like a trapped rodent surveying its cage.

As he lit the cigar, Warren said, "I have your record here." He tapped with a beautifully manicured nail on a pile of papers before him. "Five years for jewel robbery ... now this." He leaned forward and stared searchingly at Martha. "Mrs Gummrich, I must tell you the Judge will be influenced by your record. I could ask him to sentence you to ten years."

Martha cowered. Her fat flesh quivered. Ten years on that awful food! She now longed for the imaginary death pill about which she had boasted to Henry.

Warren blew a rich-smelling wreath of cigar smoke around him.

"But I could persuade the Judge to deal leniently with you." He poked his cigar in Martha's direction. "When you were arrested, you said Robins killed Mrs Lewis. Frankly, this is all I am interested in. I want to convict this man for murder. If you are prepared to give evidence against him, I can promise you that you will get a three-year sentence instead of a certain ten-year sentence. Of course you must decide for yourself. Are you prepared to become a witness for the prosecution?"

Martha didn't hesitate.

"Yes," she said.

Steve Harmas sauntered into Patty Shaw's office and smiled at her.

"How do you like my beautiful suntan?" he asked. "If I wasn't such a respectably married man, I would kiss you."

"That's nice to know," Patty said. "I'm sorry about that, but if you really feel in need of kissing anyone, go in there and kiss the bear." She rolled her pretty eyes. "The guy who coined that phrase about a bear and a boil was dead right."

Harmas shrugged.

"Don't let it worry you, Patty, dear. Do me a favour, will you? I had a bet with Max the other week about how tall you are. Stand up a second. I just want to check."

Patty giggled.

"That one's got whiskers on it. I stand up and get my bottom pinched. Go talk to Maddox."

"Miss Shaw ... I think you are getting a little worldly," Harmas said, looking shocked. "The idea never crossed my mind."

"Get in there and do some work."

Harmas looked sad, shook his head and entered Maddox's office.

Maddox glared at him.

"Have you found that necklace?"

Harmas lowered himself into the visitor's chair.

"No."

"What the hell's going on?" Maddox demanded. "I've got the claim in. I told you ... "

Harmas raised his hand. He took from his pocket an envelope and handed it across the desk.

"Look at that, then we can talk."

Snorting, one hand rumpling his hair, Maddox read Harmas' report. Then he lit a cigarette from the butt of the one he was smoking and sat back.

"I don't give a damn who killed Lisa Lewis," he said. "All I'm interested in is the Esmaldi necklace. It's got to be found. So okay, Lewis is fooling around with a Vietnamese. Terrell and you think Lewis engineered his wife's murder. That doesn't interest me! You think Lewis had the necklace ... that does interest me. Get back to Paradise City and take with you as many of your men as you think you will need. From now on, you don't take your eyes off Lewis or his Vietnamese tart. This could be the only chance of recovering the necklace. If I have to pay out, everyone in this office, including you, will have pains in their asses. Do I make myself plain?"

"Beautifully," Harmas said. "Okay, leave it to me."

As he left Maddox's office, Harmas caught Patty bending over a filing cabinet. Her sharp squeal made Maddox lift his head and frown.

Before Patty could find something heavy enough to throw at him, Harmas was half-way to the elevator.

Three days after Harry's visit to the Saigon Restaurant, he telephoned Tania, asking if they could meet.

"Yes," Tania said. "I will be at the apartment at three." There was a wooden sound to her voice that bothered Harry.

"Is there something wrong?" he asked uneasily, but found that she had hung up.

He had scarcely slept for the past three nights, thinking of her and longing for the comfort of her slim, beautiful body.

Nurse Helgar had gone with a promise, once the will had been proved, that she would receive ten thousand dollars for services rendered. She had accepted this promise with a slight nod of her head and had stared at Harry, conveying her dislike for him. He was glad to be rid of her. He had made arrangements to sell the house, warning To-To and the rest of the staff that he would be making changes. It irritated him that none of them showed concern. To-To said in his prim guttural English that he would be leaving at the end of the week as he had already had an offer which suited him. He too gave Harry a cold stare of dislike.

Unaware that Steve Harmas was following him, Harry arrived at Tania's apartment just after three o'clock. Usually when he arrived, the door would be thrown open and Tania would rush into his arms, but there was no answer to his ring on the bell, and frowning, wondering if she was there, he opened the door with his key.

"Tania?"

From the bedroom, he heard her voice.

"I am here."

He closed the front door and walked through the living-room, down the short corridor to the bedroom. He pushed the door open.

Tania was sitting before the mirror of the dressing-table. She was wearing a white wrap and she was filing her fingernails.

As Harry entered, she looked up, her face expression-less.

"Hello, Harry."

Oh, God! he thought, she is still unhappy. He wanted her. He wanted to lie with her and feel her reactions to his love-making, but he could see from the expression in the black almond-shaped eyes this was not going to happen. A wave of frustrated impatience ran through him.

"Anything wrong?" he asked, closing the door.

She looked away.

"Do you wish to make love?" she asked in a quiet, flat voice.

"Tania! Is there anything wrong?"

"Do you wish to make love?" she repeated.

He was tempted to throw her across the bed and use her as he longed to use her, but he restrained himself.

"Is that all you imagine I care about? Tania ... I love you ... what's wrong?"

He sat on the foot of the bed, looking at her. "Love? *You* love *me*?" She put down the nail file, stood up and walked to the door. "I want to talk to you, please." She went out and walked slowly, her hands hanging limply by her side, into the living-room.

Now what? Harry thought angrily. He was sorry she had left the bedroom. Once he had her in his arms, lying on the bed, he was sure he could have melted her. Now, damn it! he had lost his chance.

He followed her into the living-room. She was sitting in one of the big, comfortable chairs, holding her wrap closely to her.

"Please ... " She waved to a chair away from her.

"What is all this, Tania?" Harry said, but he sat down. He just failed to keep the edge of impatience from his voice.

"I want to talk about us, Harry. You said if you married me, you would lose all your wife's money."

So that was it, Harry thought. I imagined I had got over that goddamn hurdle.

"Yes, darling," he said. "There's no way out ... I shall have a lot of money ... we can be happy together. I can give you everything you want ... you have only to ask." He forced a smile.

"But you promised me that if you were free, you would marry me."

He felt a sudden angry urge to shout at her: "Do you imagine you or any other woman is worth two hundred million dollars? Are you that stupid?" But he restrained himself. He said nothing.

Tania sat looking at him. Two tears trickled down the perfect, satin-like skin.

"She warned me ... I wouldn't believe her," she said, her voice unsteady.

Harry stiffened.

"What are you talking about?" he demanded, feeling a sudden cold chill run through him. "*Her*? Who do you mean?"

Tania touched her tears away with a finger.

"Tania! What's got into you?" He jumped to his feet and stood over her. "Stop this! I love you ... I need you ... I want you. Why are you behaving like this?"

She looked up at him and he was stricken by the despair in her glistening black eyes.

"You don't know the meaning of love. She warned me."

Harry made an exasperated gesture. He returned to his chair and sat down.

"Have you gone out of your mind?" His voice now was sharp and angry. "She? Her? Who the hell are you talking about?"

"Your wife," Tania said softly.

Harry felt a rush of blood to his face.

"Just what is this?" he said, leaning forward, his hands on his knees, his face tight with anger.

"She knew about us, Harry," Tania said, huddling back in her chair and staring down at her trembling hands. "She had you watched. Every time we met at the restaurant and here, some man was taking notes. The morning before you went to that meeting in 'Frisco, she came to see me."

Harry sat back limply.

"Lisa! Came to see *you*?"

"Yes. Her Japanese chauffeur wheeled her into the restaurant and we met in the private room where we two meet. She told me she knew about our affair as she called it. She knew you left the house at night to meet me. There was nothing she didn't know about us. I was so worried for you. I thought because of me she would divorce you and you would lose all her money. I didn't know what to say to her, but I needn't have worried. She said I would never hold you. She sat in the wheelchair, staring at me. 'You don't know my husband as I know him,' she said. 'He has never loved me. He is incapable of love ... he only loves money.'"

"I don't believe a word of this," Harry said, his face white. "I think you're making this up!"

Tania touched her cheek with the back of her hand, wiping away a tear.

"Please listen and please believe," she said. "Your wife was sitting there so pinched, so ugly with her angry eyes, facing me. Then she told me she planned to kill herself because she was burning ... those were her words ... burning. Now she could no longer have any sex with you she didn't want to live. I could understand and I even felt sorry for her, but she didn't want my sorrow. She was very hateful. 'You will never marry him, you yellow whore,' she said to me. 'I am going to alter my will. He will have nothing if he marries you and knowing him as I know him, he won't marry you as soon as he has read my will.'" Tania paused, looking down at her hands. "I didn't know then that she was lying to me: it was only when you told me that I realised she had already altered her will. Otherwise, I wouldn't have done it."

Harry felt his mouth turn dry.

"Done it? Done ... what?"

Tania made a little movement of despair.

"You see, Harry, I began to wonder if what she had said about you was true. When she left, I thought and thought. There was this chance that if you had to choose between me and all that money, you would choose the money. I didn't want to believe it and I did so want to live with you as your wife."

"What are you trying to tell me?" Harry said hoarsely.

"It was really very easy," Tania went on. "I decided to safeguard our future. She had told me she was going to kill herself. She was suffering. I knew where the key to the patio door was ... "

"Good God!" Harry pushed back his chair, his heart hammering. "Are you telling me it was you who killed her?"

She looked at him: her eyes were like dull glass.

"Of course. She died quickly. She never woke up. It was while I was leaving the room I remembered the necklace. It seemed dreadful to me that such a beautiful necklace should go to a museum. I knew how to open the safe ... so I opened it."

She got to her feet and moved across the room while Harry watched her, petrified. She opened a drawer and took out the Esmaldi necklace. She dropped it on the floor by his feet.

"When I put it on and looked at myself in the mirror, I didn't see myself," she said. "I saw only her with that hooked nose and that pinched face, sneering at me. It was a mistake to have taken it. It was a mistake to have killed her because she was right about you, Harry. Now please leave me. Take the necklace and I hope you enjoy your money."

Without looking at him, she left the room and Harry heard her make her way to the bedroom, enter and close the door.

He had no idea how long he sat in the armchair, motionless, wondering what he should do. Should he inform the police? He knew a man had been arrested for

Lisa's murder. Should he leave things as they were? Should he get on the yacht and go off into the blue and never come back to Paradise City? This seemed to him to be his best solution. He had all the money in the world ... he could do what he liked ... go where he liked. He thought of Tania creeping into Lisa's bedroom, the bronze statuette in her hand and smashing it down on the sleeping woman's unprotected face, and he shuddered. He could never touch Tania again, yet he could not bring himself to betray her to the police. No ... the best thing was to act the part of the stricken husband, get on the yacht and sail away. Why should he worry about a thug with a record, who was known to be vicious?

As he was about to get to his feet, a band of sunlight came through the half-drawn curtains and fell directly on the Esmaldi diamonds. They came to life, like white hot stars, bursting with brilliance, dazzling him. He stared down at them. A museum would have them under glass for a gaping queue of morbid tourists to gloat over. The necklace would be a tremendous attraction once it was known it belonged to one of the richest women in the world who had been savagely murdered. The necklace was insured for three hundred and fifty thousand dollars. Harry hesitated. How stupid it would be to let the museum have this fabulous necklace. Three hundred and fifty thousand dollars! Tania would never dare say anything. The thing to do was to get rid of the necklace. Yes ... he would be out of his mind not to claim for all that money. He would drop the necklace into the sea and take the insurance money. He reached down and with an unsteady hand, he picked up the necklace. He didn't pause to think that he was now worth two hundred million dollars and he could now buy any number of necklaces every bit as beautiful and as costly as the Esmaldi diamonds. All he could think of right then was that he had the chance to collect all that insurance money and he was going to do it.

He dropped the necklace in his pocket and stood up. As

he made his way to the door, he heard a thud . . . the sound of something heavy dropping to the floor.

Instantly, he became alarmed. Had the police arrived? Was some stranger in the apartment? No, it was Tania, he assured himself. What was she doing? Then he heard a sound that made the hairs on the nape of his neck stiffen: a low, shuddering moan.

He ran blindly down the corridor and pushed open the bedroom door. He paused in the doorway as he saw Tania, lying face down on the floor by the bed.

"Tania?"

She made a slight movement. Harry ran to her, caught hold of her and turned her over. She rolled limply on to her back. The wooden handle of a kitchen knife grew out of her slim body.

"Tania!"

Her eyelids lifted and she looked at him, then the eyes glazed and became fixed. He caught hold of the knife handle and pulled the knife from her body. Immediately blood began to pour from her, over his shoes, making a sticky, horrifying mess on his hands. He reared back.

The glazed, sightless eyes told him she was dead. Shuddering, he dropped the knife, seeing blood now on the sleeve of his jacket.

All he could think of was to get out of this place . . . to get away. He paused long enough to wipe his hand free of blood on his handkerchief which he dropped, then he left the apartment.

Steve Harmas, who had been watching the apartment block, saw Harry as he came out and saw the bloodstains on his jacket. He slid out of his car and started towards Harry.

"Hey! You!"

Harry stared at him, panicked, spun around and ran. He ran the wrong way. He darted across the busy highway. A speeding car had no chance of avoiding him. Moving at over seventy miles an hour, the car hit Harry and threw him high into the air. A following car, also driving at speed, again hit Harry as he thudded on to the road.

That was the end of Harry.

Al Barney finished his drink and set the glass down with a sigh of content.

"Well, mister, I guess that's it," he said. "You know something? It's getting late. It's time for my dinner."

"What happened to the gang?" I asked.

Al shrugged his meaty shoulders.

"They're still inside. I hear Martha's lost sixty pounds."

"And Johnny?"

"They couldn't hook him to the murder rap. When they found the Esmaldi necklace in Harry's pocket, they decided Harry and Tania had fixed Lisa, and then had quarrelled over the necklace. They finally decided that Harry had murdered Tania and was taking off with the necklace when the car hit him. Maddox got most of the praise and he loved it. Johnny drew five years."

"And Gilda?"

"She drew two. Could be out any time now."

"And the Esmaldi necklace?"

"The Fine Arts Museum got it. It's drawing big crowds."

We eyed each other, then Al grinned.

"I know what you're thinking, mister, I can see it in your eyes. You're thinking I'm telling you a pack of lies. The way you are reasoning is this: how can this fat slob know more than the cops know? How did he know Harry didn't kill Tania?" He belched gently, still grinning. "As I told you, I'm a guy with an ear to the ground. People tell me things that they didn't tell the cops. Anna Woo is a pal of mine. She overheard everything that went on in Harry's love-nest and she told me. This is strictly between you and me. It is all water under the bridge now. No point in telling the cops." He looked across at Sam and made a special signal. Sam came over with the final check. I paid and tipped him.

Al got heavily to his feet.

"I'm glad to have met you, mister. I guess we had better put on our separate feed bags. Anytime you want a little information about this City, you know where to find me."

I slipped him fifty dollars which he snapped up the way a lizard snaps up a fly.

"Sad little story, wasn't it?" he said.

I said it was and left him.

>>> If you've enjoyed this book and would like to discover more great vintage crime and thriller titles, as well as the most exciting crime and thriller authors writing today, visit: >>>

The Murder Room
Where Criminal Minds Meet

themurderroom.com